"KLUV, you're on the air."

"I have a message for Mr. McKay...."

The hairs on the back of Gabby's neck stood at attention. Maybe it was the voice synthesizer the caller used...maybe it was the menacing tone. Either way, Gabby's gut twisted. "Yes?"

"Tell the Yankee if he knows what's good for him, he'll go home."

Her heart thudded. "Who is this?"

"Just know, Mr. McKay, nobody wants you here."

The line went dead. Gabby quickly queued up a set of songs, despite her trembling hands. "That was a threat, Mr. McKay. I think we should call the sheriff."

He shook his head. "That wasn't a direct threat. I'll call the sheriff later, but don't hold your breath on him being able to do anything."

But the call unnerved her. Attacks. Vandalism. Now this threat. What was happening to Mystique?

What was going on with KLUV?

Books by Robin Caroll

Love Inspired Suspense

Bayou Justice
Bayou Corruption
Bayou Judgment
Bayou Paradox
Bayou Betrayal
Framed!
Blackmail
Dead Air

ROBIN CAROLL

is the author of Deep South mysteries to inspire your heart. Her passion has always been to tell stories to entertain others. Her books have been finalists and placed in such contests as Book of the Year, Bookseller's Best Award and *RT Book Reviews'* Reviewers' Choice Award. She is the past president of American Christian Fiction Writers and currently serves as the conference director. She is a presenter and part of the faculty at several writing conferences, in addition to judging a variety of literary contests.

When she isn't plotting out her next book, Robin enjoys scrapbooking, reading and spending time with her husband of twenty years and their three daughters at home—in the South, where else? You can find Robin on the Web at www.robincaroll.com.

DEAD AIR

ROBIN CAROLL

Steeple
Hill®

Published by Steeple Hill Books™

STEEPLE HILL BOOKS

Steeple
Hill®

Recycling programs
for this product may
not exist in your area.

ISBN-13: 978-0-373-44386-4

DEAD AIR

Printed in U.S.A.

Brothers, I do not consider myself yet to have taken hold of it. But one thing I do: forgetting what is behind and straining toward what is ahead, I press on toward the goal to win the prize for which God has called me heavenward in Christ Jesus.

—*Philippians* 3:13, 14

To Ronie and Dineen—the CPs of my heart.
I can't imagine writing without you.
Love y'all!

Acknowledgments:

My most heartfelt gratitude to. . .

Editors Elizabeth Mazer and Tina James, who
inspire me with their vision and dedication.

Mentor and dear friend Colleen Coble, who never
steers me wrong. I love ya.

My first readers: Camy, Cara, Cheryl, Krystina,
Lisa and Trace, for invaluable input and support.
I appreciate you so much.

My family for continued encouragement:
Mom, Papa, Bek, Krystina, BB, Robert, Bubba,
Lisa, Brandon and Rachel, Bill and Connie,
and all the rest! My love to all.

Emily, Remington and Isabella—my precious
girls—you are my greatest inspirations and my
greatest gifts from God. I love you so much.

Case—you complete me. Love always, ME

All glory to my Lord and Savior, Jesus Christ.

ONE

"This is Gabby Rogillio. Thank you for tuning in and sharing your love stories. Join me again tonight at ten. Until then, live and love well, Mystique." She clicked off the on-air button, queued KLUV's station identification announcement, slipped off the headset and glanced at the clock again.

Where was Howard? The early-morning deejay should've reported at six, yet she hadn't seen hide nor hair of him, and it was eight. She'd called his house several times, to no avail. Was he sick? *Lord, I hope not.* The fast-approaching-fifty Howard had just gotten over a nasty spring allergy attack. Early March in Mississippi always seemed to trigger everyone's allergies.

But this morning was important. Robert Ellison, owner of the station, had called a meeting. A mandatory one. In all the years she'd worked for KLUV, he'd never done such a thing. And it had to be important to call the meeting at nine on a Friday morning.

She pushed the buttons to loop the commercials and call numbers, giving her almost fifteen full minutes until she had to queue up again, then grabbed her coffee cup. The morning news reporter would be in soon. Until he came, she'd just have to wing it.

A hum filled the corridor to the break room, and the overhead lights flickered. She'd have to remind the station's manager, Eric, to have the fluorescent bulbs replaced.

Bam! Bam! Bam!

She turned the corner, the hairs on the nape of her neck standing at attention. The station's back door batted in the breeze coming off the Gulf.

"Good morning."

Startled, Gabby spun around.

Kevin Duffy, the early-morning newsman, loped down the hall. His bright red hair stuck up all over in contrast to the black jeans hanging loosely off his hips. It never ceased to amaze Gabby that he had the smooth voice of gilded gold, but the appearance of a young lion. A tall stranger, decked out in a black suit, stood beside Kevin.

Her heart hiccupped, but this reaction had nothing to do with being surprised.

The man had amazing eyes. Were they hazel or more gold? Who was he? New to town, that much was for certain. He had a totally different demeanor than the men in Mystique. This stranger was more…suave, debonair, cultured. He smiled, a single dimple twinkling under the hall's humming lights.

She tore her gaze from the man back to Kevin. "You scared the daylights out of me."

"Sorry." He hitched a thumb toward the man. "This is Clark McKay."

Gabby nodded at the handsome man and forced a smile. "Mr. McKay."

Robert had been making noise about wanting to sell the station and leave town, but she'd thought he'd only been rambling. Then he'd announced he'd found a buyer. Mr. McKay. Was that the reason for the mandatory meeting? *Please, God, help me.* New management could very well mean she could say goodbye to the hope of her show being syndicated. Scratch that— she could be out of a job. How would she afford the down payment on *her* house on Bridges Street if she lost her job or had to take a pay cut?

Searching for any distraction, Gabby glanced toward the gaping rear entrance and then looked at Kevin. "You left the back door open."

"I didn't come in that way."

March morning sunbeams peeked around the edges of the opening, teasing Gabby with their bright rays. While she loved being the ten-to-six disc jockey, the harsh morning sun killed her attuned-to-nighttime eyes. "Then who did? It's open."

"Dunno." Kevin gave a shrug, his locks brushing against his shoulder.

Pivoting, she reached for the swinging door, then stopped before she grabbed the knob. Slivers of wood stuck out from the door frame—the knob hung askew. This wasn't just a door ajar. This was a break-in.

Gabby nudged the door open with her toe.

And sucked in air as her heart caught in her throat.

Howard Alspeed lay on the gravel, a red circle in his chest spreading like a bull's-eye. Adjacent to him, sprawled out on the stairs lay Robert Ellison. Neither man moved.

Shock froze her to the spot. She gasped for air and blinked several times. This couldn't be happening.

She dropped to her knees and laid trembling fingers against Howard's throat.

Nothing. "Noooo!" She placed the pads of her hands just below his sternum and pressed. Once. Twice. A third time.

She tilted back his head and opened his mouth.

Mr. McKay appeared at her side. He checked Howard's pulse.

Gabby bent to place her mouth over Howard's. Mr. McKay pulled her back. "Let me."

Her hands trembled as she let him take her place.

She swallowed against a dry mouth and scrambled to Robert's side. His pulse was strong and regular, but he didn't stir. His head lay against the corner of the bottom concrete step, blood pooling beneath. She touched his face. "Robert, Robert."

No response.

Kevin hovered over her. "We need to call the police. There's a gun."

Sure enough, a handgun lay inches from Robert's hands. What did that mean?

She patted Robert's shoulder. "We need to call an ambulance. And Sheriff McGruder."

Mr. McKay continued to perform CPR on Howard. No response. Tears spilled from her face.

Poor Howard, he'd been with the station since Robert bought it—he was as much of an icon of KLUV as anyone. "I'm so sorry," she whispered as tears soaked her cheeks.

The morning newsman cleared his throat. "I'll call McGruder and ask for an ambulance."

Gabby swiped a sleeve across her face. She stood, wobbling a bit. "Let me call the sheriff." She pointed at Kevin. "You stay with them."

She rushed inside, her heart thumping hard. She washed her hands quickly, a lump lodging in her throat as she watched Howard's blood trickle down the drain. Tears threatened to spill again, but she couldn't break down. Not now. She dried her hands, strode to the reception area and lifted the phone. After punching in the number to the sheriff's office, Gabby pinched the bridge of her nose. Mystique didn't even have 911 capabilities yet.

"Sheriff McGruder." His voice sounded like gravel in a barrel.

"It's Gabby Rogillio at KLUV, Sheriff." She swallowed, forcing the panic from her voice. "Howard Alspeed has been shot. And Robert Ellison is unconscious. We need an ambulance."

"What? Wh— Never mind. I'll call it in. Don't touch anything. I'm on my way." He barked orders harder than a Doberman after a petty thief. Good thing the sheriff's office was only a block away, the hospital only three.

The phone went silent in her hand. Silence…dead air! She tossed the receiver back on its base and rushed into the studio. Sure enough, her loop had ended and nothing but silence filled the airwaves. Gabby quickly grabbed a previously recorded segment of her show and queued it up, not bothering to explain on-air. How could she?

She shut the studio door just as the front door lock disengaged with an echoing click. Gabby jumped, then let out a long breath as station manager Eric Masters waltzed inside.

"Morning, Gabby. It's a beautiful day—" He cut off abruptly and studied her. His wet-from-the-shower hair lifted from the blast of the air conditioner. "What happened?"

"Oh, Eric. Howard's been shot and Robert's unconscious."

His eyes widened. "When? Where?"

She shook her head, struggling to push the words past the mountainous lump in her throat. "The back door was wide-open. Sheriff's on his way. So is the ambulance."

"Did you see anything?" He set his briefcase on the desk and moved around her toward the hall, shoving his hands into the pockets of his slacks.

"Nothing. Kevin's on the back steps with them. Mr. McKay is there, too—he's doing CPR."

Eric rubbed his clean-shaven chin. "I'll check it out."

"Sheriff McGruder said not to touch anything."

"I'm not. Just gonna look around and see if anything's missing." Eric took two steps down the corridor.

She bit her bottom lip, pushing down the panic knotted in her gut from seeing Howard. And poor Robert, the man she looked up to like a second father… Well, her heart ached.

Eric didn't look back at her, only continued to stride down the hall.

The front door swung open, letting sunlight spill into the station. Gabby blinked a few times until her eyes adjusted.

"Gabby." Sheriff McGruder nodded at her. His tall, lithe frame wore the standard uniform well.

"Sheriff."

"EMS should be here any minute. Where's the crime scene?" No polite exchanges—all business.

"Back door. Come on." She moved around the desk and took one step down the hall, the sheriff silently following.

Tears clogged her throat as she led the way down the hall. A siren wailed outside, followed by the crunch of tires on gravel.

Eric joined them in the corridor, leaning against the wall and crossing his arms over his chest. "Sheriff, I've looked over the offices. Nothing appears to be missing."

"Y'all stay here while I secure the scene and direct the paramedics." The sheriff moved to the back door and stepped outside.

Kevin and Mr. McKay entered, faces long. Gabby raised a brow. Mr. McKay shook his head. "Is there a place I can wash up?"

"I'll take you." Kevin moved toward the hallway. "I called Mrs. Ellison," he mumbled over his shoulder.

Long moments passed with no one willing to break the uncomfortable silence. Each apparently lost in their own grief and thoughts.

What had he gotten himself into?

Clark studied the people around him. While the men paced or worried the carpet with their toes, Clark's attention was drawn to the woman deejay…Gabby. Such a take-charge attitude, yet looking very soft and vulnerable. Something about her drew him in.

With the nine-o'clock hour approaching, the other employees trickled in.

"Hey, y'all," a brunette college-age girl hollered out.

Gabby turned and rushed toward her. "Oh, Ellen. We've been hit with a horrible tragedy."

The girl's eyes widened. "What kind of tragedy?"

Gabby wrapped an arm around the young part-time receptionist's waist and quietly explained. She kept her voice soft and tone low…so sensitive to the young girl's horror. Just when Gabby got Ellen a cup of coffee and dabbed her tears, a tall, graying-haired man looped down the hall.

"Gabby, what's going on?"

She turned. "David," she all but whispered. Gabby disengaged herself from the girl and gave the man a quick hug, whispering in his ear what had occurred.

He mumbled under his breath as Gabby leaned toward him, her hand lying on his forearm. After she finished talking with him, he excused himself to the studio, taking charge of the on-air segments.

When Mitch Brown, introduced as the part-time studio technician, arrived moments later, she again broke the news with softness and genuine concern.

The gentle manner in which she informed her coworkers of what had transpired sparked flames of admiration in Clark's chest. He barely had met the woman, and already she'd snagged his attention.

The back door opened with a creak.

"I need to ask some questions." The local sheriff stood just inside the doorway, whipping out his little notebook. He licked the tip of his pencil, then shot his gaze around the hall. "Who found this door open?"

"Gabby did," Kevin volunteered.

"Well, only because I heard the banging." She squared her shoulders as she spoke. Her long, dark hair hung over her shoulders, cascading like a waterfall, contrasting with her pale skin. She was certainly striking, but she'd definitely gone into the right line of work. Her husky voice seeped under his skin, warm and hypnotic.

"Uh-huh. Did you see the door open, too?" The sheriff stared at Kevin, pencil poised over the notebook.

"Yeah. When I came in." Kevin shifted his weight from one foot to the next.

"Which was what time?"

"I report at eight."

"You were late." Gabby crossed her arms over her chest.

"How late were you?" the sheriff asked.

"Only about ten minutes or so." Kevin tossed Gabby a stare that would freeze flames. "I had to meet Mr. McKay."

"Right. I'll get to you in a minute." The sheriff gave Clark a glance that traveled up and down his length. Clark fought hard not to squirm under the scrutiny. Why would the sheriff question them together? Back in Philly, people were separated and questioned. Maybe they did it different in small towns down South.

Or maybe they weren't accustomed to dealing with a murder.

The lawman focused his attention back on Kevin. "Did you see anything when you drove up? Anything out of the ordinary?"

"Not that I noticed." He ducked his head, his freckled face turning pink. "I was rushing to meet Mr. McKay. I was running late, remember?"

"Uh-huh." The sheriff tapped the pencil's eraser against his chin. "And just why were you running late?"

Kevin's already ruddy complexion reddened. "I was out late last night and overslept."

"Can anyone verify that?"

His face turned a deeper shade of crimson. "Yes. My girl-friend, Mona. She's still at my apartment."

"Mona who?"

"Kingston."

The sheriff scribbled in his notebook, then asked for Kevin's address and home phone number, as well as that of Mona.

Kevin hung his head as he gave the information.

The sheriff turned to the station manager. "What about you?"

"What about me?" Eric shifted his weight from one foot to the other. "I didn't know anything until I got here and Gabby told me, after she'd already called you."

"Where were you this morning?"

"Home. Having breakfast and getting ready for work."

"Can anyone verify that you were at home?" The sheriff glanced up from his notebook.

Eric tightened his jaw. "No. I live alone."

"Did you stop anywhere on the way in? Talk to anyone on the phone?"

"No."

"I see." The sheriff flipped a page in his notebook and nodded at Gabby. "You were apparently here—did you hear anything?"

"No, I was in the studio."

"You didn't hear a gunshot mere yards away? And the marks in the gravel out there indicates there was a struggle of some sort."

She clenched and unclenched her hands. "The studio's soundproof."

The lawman settled his stare on her. "I understand that. Just trying to determine if you saw or heard anything. Maybe saw Mr. Ellison or Mr. Alspeed in the hall?"

"No, I didn't see anything."

The sheriff made further notes, then turned to Clark. "Who are you, and what are you doing here?"

Straightening, he looked at the lawman head-on. "I'm Clark McKay. I was told to be here at eight this morning to meet Mr. Ellison and the station staff."

The sheriff huffed. "What about?"

How did he answer that? It seemed wrong just to blurt out the truth, considering the circumstances. "A business endeavor."

"What, exactly, does that mean?"

All eyes burned into him. Might as well tell the truth. They'd all find out soon enough. "I'm the new owner of KLUV."

Gabby gasped. Eric scowled. Kevin shrugged in that nonchalant way of his. "Cool."

The sheriff scribbled furiously in his notebook. "I see. When did this take place?"

"We finalized the paperwork two days ago."

"And where were you this morning?"

"At my house." Clark straightened. "And yes, someone can verify that. My great-aunt stopped by with homemade cinnamon buns."

Sheriff McGruder glanced at him, scraggly brows raised. "Who would your aunt be?"

"Beulah. McKay."

The lawman let out a grunt as he scribbled again. "I know her address and phone number."

The door squeaked open and a paramedic stuck his head inside. "We're taking them to the hospital now."

"Thank you." The sheriff faced the group in the hallway. "After I conclude my examination of the crime scene, I'll file my report and call each of you in to sign your statements." Sheriff McGruder pocketed his notebook.

"Wait a minute. Are we, like, suspects?" Kevin straightened, tossing off his slouch like a bad suit jacket.

"Right now, *everyone* is suspect."

TWO

DOA. Dead on arrival.

Gabby had caught a glimpse of Howard as EMS loaded him into the ambulance, still performing CPR. No response, and he'd been down for a long time. She knew it—he was dead.

Murdered. Gabby's heart ached like it hadn't since…well, in a long time.

She gathered her purse and stormed into the bright parking lot, climbed into her SUV and steered toward the hospital. Sending up a silent prayer for Robert, she ignored the tranquil beauty of her town. Instead, questions of who would want to hurt Howard and Robert plagued her. Lifting her cell phone, she punched in the speed-dial number for her best friend Imogene.

"Hello." Imogene's calm tone steadied Gabby's thrumming heart immediately.

"Oh, Immy, Howard was shot at the station this morning. Robert's unconscious. They were taken away by ambulance. I'm on my way to the hospital now." She struggled to keep the tears at bay.

"Great day in the morning! A shooting? I'll call Dr. Wright and tell him I'll be a little late. I'll meet you in the emergency room."

Gabby whipped into the hospital's lot, parked and jogged

past the automatic glass doors. She stopped at the nurses' desk. "I'm here with Robert Ellison and Howard Alspeed."

The nurse nodded. "Someone will be with you shortly."

Gabby wandered into the waiting room. An elderly lady with an ice pack on her arm offered her a shaky smile. Gabby returned it, then headed to the coffee station in the corner. She lifted the carafe and peered inside. The coffee resembled sludge and didn't smell much better. She shoved the pot back on the warmer.

"Miss?"

She turned and faced the man in scrubs. "Yes?"

"Are you with Howard Alspeed?"

"Yes." She walked to the doctor on wobbly knees. "I am."

"I'm sorry, but we were unable to revive him. His heart was hit by the bullet."

No words formed. Tears burned her eyes. She nodded.

"We'll let you know about Mr. Ellison as soon as we can." He rushed down the hallway toward the treatment rooms.

It was official. Howard had been murdered.

"Gabby."

Turning, she spied Immy and rushed to her, letting the comfort of her friend's embrace warm her. Together, they plopped onto metal chairs.

"What happened?"

As Gabby relayed the morning's events, her own feelings mirrored in the expressions that crossed her best friend's face—shock, a trace of fear, then outrage.

Imogene's eyes were wide in her full face. "Great day in the morning! What do the police say?"

"Say?" Gabby shook her head. "They don't say anything. McGruder doesn't seem to have the first clue."

"The police don't have even one suspect?"

"Not that they're sharing. Aside from all of us who work at

the station, apparently." Gabby hugged herself, willing the image of Howard's dead face to flee. "Oh, and Mr. McKay."

"Who's he?"

"The new owner of the station. Robert had asked everyone to come in for a meeting this morning." Her heart thudded. "I'm guessing he was going to make the official announcement."

The ground slipped out beneath Gabby's feet. Visions of the house on Bridges Street flickered across her mind. She'd been saving for the down payment for a couple of years and refused to consider not being able to buy the house. But now everything was thrown into turmoil. The station changing hands on top of the murders… What if she lost her job? Mystique, Mississippi, wasn't exactly the Garden of Eden of employment opportunities. Would Mr. McKay bring in his own staff? What would happen to all her plans and dreams?

No, the house, *her* house, was not merely a pipe dream—she would see it through to reality. She'd own her antebellum home if it was the last thing she did. Not to make light of Howard's murder and Robert's injuries—definitely not—but inside she felt like more than Howard had just died.

"Who would do such a thing?"

Gabby groaned as she returned her thoughts to the horrors of the morning. "I just can't imagine anyone wanting to harm either Howard or Robert."

Immy shifted in the chair—it gave a protesting creak in response—and stretched her legs in front of her. "The police have to know something. Or at least be *doing* something."

"If they are, McGruder's not passing along the information."

"Maybe he's working angles he can't share with anyone. But I still say Mystique isn't a crime metropolis." Imogene twisted her gentle face into a scowl. "I've known the townies for years, have treated everyone here at least once—none of them would do such a thing. Everyone loves Howard and Robert." As a nurse, Immy had such compassion toward everyone, even if she did walk a little on the naive side.

Gabby popped her knuckles. "We shouldn't jump to any conclusions. It could be anybody."

"Or it could be an outsider, right?"

"Right." Gabby spied one of the deputies marching down the hall. "McGruder's obviously in way over his head. Our sheriff department's big event is hauling in a drunk or two on a Saturday night."

"How was Robert?" Imogene finger-combed her bangs.

"Unconscious when he left in the ambulance."

"Let me see if I can find out anything." Imogene blinked rapidly as she rose and headed to the nurses' station.

Alone, Gabby flipped through her mental filing cabinet. Nothing made sense. Who would want to hurt Robert or Howard?

"Robert's still unconscious. They're running tests," Immy said, returning to her chair. "They do know his blood sugar level was extremely low. For a hypoglycemic, that's very bad. Could be what caused him to lose consciousness. They speculate that's what happened, and he fell on the stairs and hurt his head."

Gabby let that digest for a moment. "I just can't believe this is happening."

"I know." Immy laid an arm around Gabby's shoulders.

"Oh, Gabby. It's so awful." Amber Ellison, Robert's wife, rushed forward, sobbing.

Gabby moved out of Immy's hug just in time to catch the bawling woman. "How is he?"

"He's unconscious." Amber sniffled. "They're admitting him to ICU where they'll run more tests." She dabbed her face with a tissue. "He had to have eight stitches on the back of his head."

"I guess you heard about Howard?"

Amber's cries increased. "It's unbelievable. I don't understand."
Gabby patted the woman's shaking shoulders.

How could anyone understand such a senseless attack?

What a mess.

Clark stared at the signed papers he held. The purchase agreement between him and Robert Ellison. The one that made him sole owner and proprietor of KLUV radio station.

He tossed them into his briefcase and pushed away from his desk. Mr. Ellison was to have made the announcement to the employees this morning. Sitting in his office, surrounded by Mr. Ellison's personal effects, made Clark uneasy. Today was supposed to have been a good day, a day of excitement and one he'd anticipated.

Now he was tied up in another scandal. And after what he'd gone through in Philly, that was just about the last thing he needed.

He'd called the hospital. Robert Ellison was still unconscious. What should he do now? He had to do something. He had been ready to commit to the business he'd purchased and this town, having bought a house instead of renting, but what would happen if the media jumped all over this?

That couldn't happen. He couldn't stand the thought of going through that again. Sure he'd managed to clear his name, but his reputation had been tarnished. And he'd discovered exactly who his real friends were. Or rather, weren't.

That particular realization had been the last straw. It forced him to move somewhere life was a little slower-paced, more routine. Where he had family. The small town where his great-aunt Beulah lived, Mystique, Mississippi, had seemed to fit the bill.

Until a man had been murdered and another left unconscious.

"Knock, knock. May I come in?" Eric hovered in the doorway.

"Sure." Clark waved the station manager to one of the chairs facing his desk. "What can I help you with?"

Eric slouched into the seat. "I just wanted to talk with you about the station a bit, if I may?"

Clark tented his hands over his desk. "What's on your mind?"

"Look, I didn't know about the sale, and really don't care. It's none of my business." He shot Clark a sly grin. "Unless you plan on firing me, of course."

Clark smiled. "I don't intend to fire people. Especially key personnel."

"Good. That's a relief." Eric sat a little straighter in the chair. "I need to rearrange some of the airtime schedules to cover Howard's time slot. That is, if you want me to."

"Please. For the time being, continue to do your job as you normally have."

Eric nodded, but didn't rise. Everything about his demeanor told Clark the man had something else eating at him.

"Something you want to tell me?"

Eric met his stare. "I wanted to tell you that nobody will blame you if you backed out of the deal."

What? Clark sat forward and studied the young station manager.

"I mean, I'm sure you have a clause in the contract if you don't want to deal with all this." Eric spread his fingers. "The murder's already hit the gossip mill. Sponsors and advertisers will probably pull their money out of the station. It'd be a bad business move on anyone's part to continue with the sale." He shrugged. "I'm just saying no one will blame you if you walk away."

The argument Clark had yet to have with himself, despite the urging of his business logic. "I honestly don't know what I'm going to do just yet."

Eric nodded. "It's a hard call." He stood. "I just wanted to tell you there'd be no hard feelings if you packed up and hauled it back up North. Everyone would understand."

Haul it back North? A not-so-subtle hint that he didn't fit in here? "I appreciate your candor. I need to call my attorney and discuss the situation with him."

"Yeah, I get that. He'll probably tell you to run as fast as you can."

Clark chuckled, picturing his straight-laced attorney. "Probably."

"In the meantime, let me know if you need anything." Eric gave a mock salute and strode from the office.

Clark glanced out the window. The manager was right—he should get back to Philly and forget all about KLUV and Mystique.

But something strong inside urged him to stay put.

He shook his head. He'd figure it all out later. It was possible the sheriff would solve the case in a matter of days and then this whole mess would be behind him. That would be ideal.

Closing his briefcase, he made his way to the front door of KLUV. The police had finished their evidence-gathering and Clark had a locksmith come and repair the back door. Even so, he preferred to use the front entrance.

He waved at David Gray in the deejay booth. The kindly, laid-back man wagged fingers in return. Clark locked the front doors behind him, then headed to his car. Even though it was barely six-thirty, the sun had already set and the streets were quiet—a big contrast to the hustle and bustle he was used to. Eric was right about one thing. He didn't fit in here, yet.

Maybe once everyone knew he was now a local business owner, they'd be a bit more friendly. Not that anyone had been rude, never, but he caught the sideway glances and raised brows. They were polite to him now because of Aunt Beulah. But maybe once he became known in the community, he'd actually be accepted. On his own merit.

At least now he had a real home to go to at the end of the day. He'd moved out of the B and B yesterday, having arrived in

Mystique a week ago to check out the town. If he would uproot and put himself in culture shock, he wanted to make sure he could live in the area. And he'd liked what he'd seen. So much so that when the Realtor brought him the folio on this house and told him he'd do better to buy than rent, it hadn't taken much convincing to get him to sign on the dotted line.

His new home was an old antebellum with such character. No longer would he allow himself to get off track on what he needed. He'd moved to a place where life was slower, kinder.

As he walked over to where he'd parked, Clark made mental notes of little things he needed to add to his to-do list of renovations. When he completed the house, it'd be restored to the glory it must have possessed back in pre–Civil War days. The house had charm, and it promised him a lifetime of happiness. At least, that's what Clark chose to believe.

He stopped abruptly when he got to his car.

Apparently it would take a bit longer than expected for the locals to get used to him. One local had made the message very clear.

The letters were spray-painted across the hood of his car.

GO HOME YANKEE.

"I can't believe McGruder doesn't have any suspects other than y'all." Rayne wrinkled her aristocratically perfect nose. The youngest of the tight circle of Gabby's friends, she was the most serious and oozed confidence right down to her polished manicure. Then again, after spending several years in a Swedish finishing school, she skippy sure better have all the spit and polish her daddy had paid a small fortune to attain.

Gabby nodded absentmindedly and stifled a yawn. She'd caught a couple of hours of sleep after leaving the hospital, but still felt a little groggy. She gazed out the picture windows lining the front of Ms. Minnie's diner, allowing the serenity of the area to calm her irritations. Oak trees swayed down Shannon Street, kudzu vines crept up the trunks nearly covering the bark and drowning out the hope of new growth. Saltiness hung in the air, riding on the wings of the March winds. Mystique, Mississippi, was Southern flavor at its best, and filled Gabby's heart with pure contentment. Coming back home after the Blake Riggsdale fiasco had been the right choice. If only it didn't feel as if her dream were slowly slipping through her fingertips.

Rayne continued. "Any change in Mr. Ellison?"

"I called the hospital when I woke. He's still unconscious, but the doctors say his vitals are good. At least his blood sugar level has evened out. Immy said she'd get an update later tonight."

"I told Amber I'd bring her a sandwich when I left here."

Gabby struggled with frustration, hauling in a deep breath. The diner's door opened, the little bell tinkling overhead.

Sheriff McGruder strode inside, his cop persona intact. He glanced at the offerings of Mystique gossips and old men who had nothing better to do than spend the entire day in the diner. He stopped when his gaze lit on Gabby. He scrutinized her from lowered eyes.

Was he here just to check up on her? Heat shot up Gabby's spine. Did he *really* think of her as a suspect? Or maybe he thought she knew more than she'd said?

"What's wrong?" Concern flashed in Rayne's eyes.

Gabby gave a nod toward the sheriff as he stopped to speak to a couple of the blue-hairs by the entrance. "Sheriff McGruder. He's giving me the evil eye."

Her friend glanced at the door. "Well, I think it's just tacky that he'd show up here tonight after everything that happened. He should be working on the case." Rayne flipped her smooth, honey-colored hair over her shoulder. "And staring so openly. That's just plain *rude.*"

Gabby sighed as Ms. Minnie, owner and proprietor of the diner, sashayed over to their table, her flowery dress flowing as she moved and her feet scuffling in her house shoes. Her trademark, a dainty monogrammed handkerchief, wasn't tucked all the way into her bodice. The woman was as sweet as her homemade chocolate pies, but her sense of fashion left a *lot* to be desired.

Gabby and Rayne had barely placed their orders and watched Ms. Minnie shuffle to the kitchen when Sheriff McGruder ambled up to the table.

"How're you ladies this evening?" His gaze settled on Gabby, but she knew the politeness wasn't for her sake. He had to play nice with Rayne sitting at the table. The VanDoren name carried a lot of weight in the great state of Mississippi.

"Can I help you with something, Sheriff?" Gabby kept her tone even.

"Actually, I was wondering if you'd thought any more about the incident this morning. Do you remember anything else, now that you've had a little time to calm down and think things over?" He shoved his thumbs through the belt loops of his khaki uniform pants and widened his stance, almost rocking back on his heels. "Anything you care to share?"

So he *did* think she was holding back, as if she'd willingly let whoever attacked Robert and Howard escape charges. The breathing trick she'd mentally ordered for herself didn't work. Blood rushed to her head, drowning out the clatter of the silverware, the gossips cackling and the music from the archaic jukebox. "You know what, Sheriff? Maybe if you would do your job, you wouldn't have to waste the time of law-abiding citizens." So much for any of Rayne's poise rubbing off on her.

His leathery, tanned face twisted into a scowl, and his eyes narrowed. "Seems to me you're awfully defensive, Ms. Rogillio. Now why's that?"

"I'm not being defensive. I'm just pointing out the obvious."
Her heart pounded so hard it nearly cracked her ribs.

"Uh-huh. I see."

His radio crackled to life. "Sheriff, we have a report of vandalism at the KLUV station."

Gabby perked up. Vandalism?

"Any witnesses?" he asked into his radio and moved a step away from their table.

"No, sir. A car was spray-painted. Driver called it in."

"Really?" McGruder moved another step away. Gabby had to lean to keep up with the conversation.

"Yes, sir. He'll be waiting at the scene for you. A McKay. Mr. Clark McKay. Says you met him this morning."

Gabby gasped.

McGruder frowned in her direction. "Copy that, Marcie. I'm on my way." He gave a curt nod to Gabby and Rayne. "Just remember, if you *do* think of anything, call me immediately."

No kidding? Gee, the man should get on the application list for NASA.

Gabby only nodded, too busy digesting what she'd heard to reply.

Someone had messed with Mr. McKay's car? Could it be connected to the attack on Robert and Howard?

THREE

Yet another benefit of living in a small town—police make it in record time. Back in Philly he'd have been waiting at least thirty minutes to an hour. Here, it only took ten minutes from the time he placed the call for the sheriff's car to squeal to a stop beside his.

McGruder ambled toward him, toting a flashlight despite the streetlight's bright glare. "Is this all the damage, Mr. McKay?"

"All that I noticed." Clark frowned. "You think there could be more?"

"Couldn't rightly say." The sheriff shrugged. "I called for a tow truck. Once I'm done collecting evidence, he'll tote it over to the auto shop and have the mechanic check it out."

The tow truck arrived just a minute later.

McGruder looked at Clark. "I'll file a report and get out here when it's daylight to take some scene pictures."

Guess that was the best he could hope for. "I appreciate that, Sheriff."

"Need a ride back to town?"

Somehow, the idea of riding in the cruiser with McGruder was akin to visiting a dentist for a root canal. "Actually, I hoped the tow shop might also rent cars."

"We do. I can bring you back with me to pick one up," the

tow truck operator, who had the name *Fred* stitched to the front pocket of his uniform, said as he completed securing Clark's car.

"Then I'll find you tomorrow after I write up my report." McGruder turned to Fred again. "Tell Lou I need a report if he finds any other tampering."

"Will do, Sheriff." Fred nodded to Clark. "You ready?"

Clark climbed into the passenger's side of the tow truck. The whole business had been concluded in less than twenty minutes. At least something was going his way. His stomach rumbled. As soon as he grabbed the rental car, he'd find something in town to eat. It'd been a long day.

And it wasn't over yet.

Gabby pushed back the empty pie plate and lifted her coffee cup. "Man, Ms. Minnie outdid herself with that one."

"It was good. I'm too full to move." Rayne shoved her plate to the center of the table.

"Good thing I have some time before my show. Need to let this food settle."

"I don't want to wait too long, though. I need to take the sandwich to Amber."

The waitress came over and topped off their cups as patrons came and went. Gabby glanced around the diner and froze as her gaze collided with that of Mr. Clark McKay's.

"He's here," she whispered.

"Who?" Rayne flicked her glance around the diner.

"Shh. Don't look. Mr. McKay."

Rayne ignored Gabby's instructions and peered about.

He stared, studying Gabby as she took a sip. She reminded herself that she shouldn't like his attention. It didn't matter how attractive she found him, gawking at her was just plain tacky. And the quickening of her traitorous heart aggravated her all the more.

Carol Ann, the waitress, sauntered over to his table, her hips revealing curves which were more attractive on a woman ten years younger. "Honey, what can I get you?" Her voice floated across the diner.

Gabby ground her teeth—could Carol Ann *be* more obvious? Her north-of-the-Mason-Dixon-Line roots showed. Almost as glaringly as her black roots against her platinum-blond hair.

"Uh, coffee, I guess. And a meat loaf sandwich," he mumbled to Carol Ann, but his gaze remained glued to Gabby. The waitress let out a loud huff and moved back toward the counter.

Just a minute later, Carol Ann returned to his table with his order. "How about a piece of pie? Ms. Minnie's pecan pie is famous down in these parts."

"Yes, fine. That will do." His voice reverberated through the diner.

The waitress smiled again, batting the eyelashes that were as fake as the Botox injections around her eyes, and strutted away.

"It may be tasteless," Rayne said with a smile on her rosebud lips, "but the man *is* handsome as all get-out, Gab."

She cut her gaze to him just as Carol Ann placed his pie in front of him. "If you don't like that, honey, you let me know and it's on the house."

He nodded, sparing a brief glance at her before darting his focus back on Gabby. What was his deal? Every nerve in her body seemed to be on full alert.

Suddenly, he shoved to his feet. Tall, the man stood well over six feet. And the muscle tone in those wide shoulders? Land sakes, he looked like some modern-day Adonis. Gabby had the overwhelming urge to fan herself.

He paused two steps from her table, his earnest stare pinning her to the spot. Time stood still. After taking the remaining strides to hover at the table, he cleared his throat. "I'm sorry to interrupt, but I'd like to buy you a cup of coffee." He didn't address either woman in particular, but his gaze remained only on Gabby.

He was as handsome as Blake, which automatically made her worry. She wouldn't let attraction put her heart at risk again. Her tongue tied.

Rayne's did not. "I see someone I need to talk to, but Gabby's free. Isn't that right, Gabby?"

"I'd really like to discuss a few things with you, if you don't mind," Clark said.

Rayne's elbow dug sharply into Gabby's side, combined with a glare. Gabby sighed and shoved to her feet. Maybe this was her chance to learn what he was really after. He was a man—he had to be after something. And she did want to learn more about his vandalism issue. "I can join you if you'd like."

He smiled slowly and nodded mutely. He waved her in front of him and then pulled out the vacant chair at his table for her. Carol Ann appeared as soon as he slipped into his seat. After she refilled his cup while she stared at him, nearly pouring coffee on his hand, she made a quick exit. He smiled across the table. "I think maybe we got off on the wrong foot."

Gabby gave a slight tilt of her head. "Did we?"

"I think so." He let out a sigh and steepled his hands. "I believe you were shocked I'd purchased KLUV."

"That's an understatement."

"Is it such a bad thing?"

Oh, his smile was deadly. Men with such disarming smiles ought to have permits for them. She focused on keeping her voice even. "You tell me. Why would an outsider be interested in a station in Mystique, Mississippi, of all places?"

"I was looking for a slower pace of living and liked Mystique from when I visited my great-aunt. I moved here from Philly." He took a bite of the pecan pie.

"What're you doing so far south?" A Yankee, that would explain the staring.

"I wanted to get away from the rat race and decided to move closer to my aunt." He smiled that killer grin again. "Mystique seems to suit me just fine."

She traced the cup's lip, choosing her next words carefully. Maybe she needed to be more direct if she wanted him to share his agenda. "Mystique's sure a long way from Philadelphia, Mr. McKay. Strange someone would just up and buy a business here without having stayed here for a spell. You haven't stayed here long before, have you?"

The smile jerked firmly back in place, hiding whatever true emotions lurked behind his gold-flecked eyes. "I've visited my aunt a lot over the years, but only a long weekend here and there." He slipped the final bite of pie between his lips.

"Mystique's not a hopping town, that's for sure." She leaned forward a fraction of an inch. "Though I'd imagine a Yankee such as yourself would have lots of plans for how to fix that."

He sat back in his chair, smiling and staring at her. Mr. Clark McKay was one cool customer. Maybe she needed to be blunt.

She smiled across the table. "Tell me, Yankee, what sparks your interest in KLUV?"

Shock marched across his face. He cleared his throat. "Like I said, I want to make Mystique my home."

"Doesn't explain your interest in the station."

"True. But I have a journalism background."

Like Blake. Fire burned in her belly. "And that qualifies you to run a station?"

He grinned. "No, but I used to own an independent newspaper. They're pretty similar."

Finally, a little background. "I suppose." Gabby rested her

chin in her hands and decided to see how forthcoming he'd be on another topic. "Sheriff McGruder was here when he got the call about your car."

A cloud dropped over his face. "I don't know what happened."

"The dispatcher said there was spray paint involved."

He nodded. "Yes. Apparently someone wanted to send a message."

"And just what would that message be?"

He gave her a wry grin. "Go home, Yankee."

Gabby sat back with a thud. "Any idea who'd do such a thing? And why?"

"I don't really know anybody in Mystique yet, outside of Aunt Beulah's friends." He chuckled. "I can't imagine one of them stocking up on spray paint."

"Probably not." She grinned and lifted a casual shoulder. Time to return to her main concern. "So, what do you think of KLUV?"

"Looks like a solid investment." He wadded up his napkin and set it on his empty plate. "I think it has a lot of potential."

A lot of potential? Gabby's stomach threatened to reverse the supper she'd just devoured. That phrase usually meant big changes. Something she couldn't fathom happening. "I think we're doing pretty well."

"I didn't mean to imply otherwise. I'm merely stating it could do better."

A big-city man changing everything…hadn't she learned not to trust men like him? "So, is this what you wanted to discuss with me? KLUV doing better?"

"No. Right now, I think it's appropriate to make an announcement of the sale. I want you to help with that."

"You kinda did. At the station." After they'd found Howard and Robert. She blinked back her tears.

"I meant publicly."

The tears dissipated completely. "As in?"

"On the air."

Her stomach knotted. "Do you think that's smart? I mean, right now? While Robert's in the hospital and Howard's…"

"I think it's the perfect time." He tented his hands over the table. "We don't want to lose any advertisers or supporters, wondering what will happen to the station if Mr. Ellison is incapacitated in the hospital."

"I see." The knot in her gut tightened.

He reached across the table and laid his hand over hers. Heat trailed up her arm. She tucked her hand into her lap. A frown marred his handsome face. "Understand I have to look out for the business. Mr. Ellison would do the same."

She plastered on a smile, knowing Robert would do no such thing. "I understand." He was her boss. She didn't have to agree with him. She just had to do what he said. "When would you like to make the announcement?"

"I was thinking tonight. Maybe around eight. After the news and weather update."

"Fine. I'll come in a little early."

Before he could reply, Rayne stood beside the table. "Gab, I've got to take this sandwich by the hospital and get back to work. You ready?"

"Yeah, I'll meet you at the truck." She drew to her feet in one fluid motion. "Thank you for the coffee. I'll see you at the station whenever you're ready." She turned and headed out the door, lifting her hand to wave as she passed the remaining townies on her way to the door.

Digging into her purse for her keys, her mind argued with her heart. Clark McKay was trouble with a capital *T,* just like Blake Riggsdale. So why did her heart continue to thump like a Jamaican melody in her chest?

* * *

Clark's attention focused on the intriguing woman until he could no longer see her from the window, then remained there on the off chance she'd return for a last, parting look.

She didn't.

With a sigh, he stood and ambled to the counter.

"She's a sweetheart, that Gabby."

Clark jerked his gaze from the window to study the white-haired woman watching him from behind the counter.

"My name's Minnie," she said as an introduction, stuffing a handkerchief back into the bodice of her flower-print dress. "That Gabby, she's something special."

"She sure is." He whispered the words, but it didn't matter. He spoke more to himself than to the proprietor of the diner.

He handed his bill to the older lady. She rang him up on the antique register. "You that new owner of the house on Bridges Street, aren't ya? Beulah's nephew?"

"Yes, ma'am."

"And I heard tell today that you'd bought KLUV from Robert."

Clark bit back a smile. Maybe the announcement wasn't as necessary as he'd thought. It seemed like small-town gossip got the word out pretty fast with or without his help. Just like Eric had warned. "That's right," he said.

"Such a tragedy," she replied with a sigh. "Both of the owners getting attacked like that today."

"Both?"

"Robert and Howard."

"Howard was an owner of KLUV?" Only Robert's name had been on the paperwork.

"Oh, yes." She gave him his change. "Right up until a few months ago."

"What happened then?"

"Oh, there was quite a to-do." Minnie spun out her tale with Southern flair. "Right here in this very café. Robert said he wanted to sell the station and Howard—" she paused, patting herself "—Howard disagreed. So Robert said he'd buy him out. Which I suppose he did, if Robert's sold the station to you. Strange thing, though—lots of strange things. The sale, those awful attacks, Robert and Howard quarreling when I've never known either man to have a harsh word for anyone." She shook her head. "You be careful over there, young man. There's something wrong there, mark my words."

After handing over a five for the tip, Clark nodded. "Yes, ma'am. I sure will."

He made a swift getaway, and slipped into his car, realizing she was right. There was something wrong. A big part of him wanted to ignore it. He was sick to death of scandal and accusations and uncovering truths ruthless people would go to great lengths to keep covered. He'd come to Mystique to slow down, to relax. And yet…once a newsman, always a newsman. And that newsman instinct was telling him that he couldn't let this drop, couldn't walk away before he'd learned what was *really* going on.

Life in Mystique might turn out to be a lot more exciting than he'd thought.

FOUR

Gabby glanced at Mr. McKay, headphones settled over his ears. It was five minutes till eight when he'd shown up, ready to make the big announcement. That she was less than enthusiastic shouldn't come across in her voice.

This was her job. Mr. McKay was her boss, no matter how much the idea bothered her.

The song ended, and she keyed up her mic. "Good evening, Mystique. Thank you for listening. This is Gabby Rogillio, playing the dedications of your heart. Before I move into the next set, as I promised you earlier, we have a very important announcement to make." She licked her lips, willing excitement into her tone. "In the studio with me tonight is Mr. Clark McKay. Welcome, Mr. McKay."

He leaned toward the mic she'd set for him. "Thank you, Gabby."

"Why don't you tell our listeners about the big KLUV announcement?"

"Certainly. I'm pleased to announce that I've purchased KLUV from Mr. Ellison."

"Mystique, I hope you all give Mr. McKay a true Southern welcome. He's from the Philadelphia area, so let's pull out the welcome rug and show him what Southern hospitality is all about." She queued the station identification tune. "After these messages, we'll get back to the dedications of your heart." She set the loop, turned off her mic and removed the headphones.

Mr. McKay did the same. "So, how do you think it went?"

She glanced at the flashing lights on the phone. "We'll see." She pressed the button and answered via speakerphone. "KLUV, you're on the air."

"Hey, Gabby, did I hear you right? A Yankee bought the station?"

She gestured for Mr. McKay to answer.

He paused for a moment, as if to gather his thoughts.

"Gabby, you there?"

She couldn't leave a caller hanging. "Sure, we're here. Mr. McKay is the new owner of KLUV. We're all very excited to start a new chapter for the station."

"But he's a Yankee, right?"

She put her smile into her voice. "Only by birth, not by choice."

The caller laughed. "Then I'll look forward to meeting him. Thanks, Gabby."

She took the next call. "KLUV, you're on the air."

"This Mr. McKay...how'd he buy the station? I heard Mr. Ellison's unconscious."

She looked to Clark again. This time, he came through.

"Mr. Ellison and I have been negotiating for days. The paperwork was finalized this week, before this incident occurred."

"Oh, hello, Mr. McKay."

"Hello." He glanced at Gabby. "I'm really looking forward to meeting everyone in Mystique and making this my home."

No response over the line. He looked to Gabby again.

She shrugged. "Do you have a dedication?"

"No, I just wanted to know what was going on."

Gabby pressed the button again. "KLUV, you're on the air."

"I have a message for Mr. McKay...."

The hairs on the back of Gabby's neck stood at attention. Maybe it was the voice synthesizer the caller used…maybe it was the menacing tone. Either way, Gabby's gut twisted. She wet her lips. "Yes?"

"Tell the Yankee if he knows what's good for him, he'll go home."

Her heart thudded. Same message that had been spray-painted on his car. "Who is this?"

"Just know, Mr. McKay, nobody wants you here."

The line went dead. Gabby quickly queued up a set of songs, despite her trembling hands.

"I had no idea so many people hated me." Clark's voice didn't waver.

"That was a threat, Mr. McKay. I think we should call the sheriff."

"And report what? The good people of Mystique don't like me? Won't accept me as a new business owner?" He shook his head. "That wasn't a direct threat. Nothing the sheriff can do."

"But it was the same threat that was spray-painted on your car. And the caller used a device to disguise his voice. Who does that unless they're up to no good?"

"I'll call McGruder later, but don't hold your breath on the sheriff being able to do anything."

But the call unnerved her. Attacks. Vandalism. Now this threat. What was happening to Mystique?

What was going on with KLUV?

Gabby took four more calls of people asking questions about Mr. McKay, or how Robert was. No more harassing callers, thank goodness. Enough was enough. She settled the headphones over her ears and leaned over her mic. "Mystique, we're all praying for Robert Ellison's full and speedy recovery. This next song is dedicated to him." She flipped the switch, and the opening bars of "He Ain't Heavy, He's My Brother" filled the studio.

"You handled that well." Mr. McKay set the headphones on the desk and stood. "Thank you."

"It's my job, right?" Her heart pounded. How could she have been so rude? To her boss, of all people?

His brows bunched. "I suppose so."

"I guess you want to get settled in Robert's office? I don't think he removed his personal effects."

"That's okay. I'll start in there on Monday. Maybe Mr. Ellison will be better then."

She clenched and unclenched her hands under the desk. "I pray so."

"Me, too." He hesitated at the door. "Well, thank you again."

She smiled, then turned back to the phones, ignoring him as he left. She sighed when he moved down the hall.

It'd been her job. But she hoped he wouldn't find any more reasons to come by for the late-night show. He was too handsome. Too charming. Too much of everything she wasn't supposed to let herself admire.

Not again.

Every pew filled to overflowing in the small community church. Clark waited until the benediction was completed before slipping out from the back row pew. He shook Pastor Lum's hand, then waited in the foyer. The message had been inspiring and well delivered, but Clark had to admit, he'd been less moved by the sermon than by the Bible reading given by Ms. Gabby Rogillio. He could listen to her voice all day…and planned to listen to it at least a little longer *this* day, if she'd agree to join him for lunch.

Several members of the congregation came to him, hands

extended, welcoming him to Mystique. He'd longed for this kind of fellowship.

"…and you must join the singles Sunday school group," said an elderly lady with glasses as dated as her muumuu dress. But Clark's attention focused over the lady's shoulder.

Gabby.

He touched the lady's shoulder softly and made his escape. Weaving around the throng of people lingering and chatting in the foyer, he hurried to her. She stood surrounded by a flock of friends. He sucked up his courage and approached her. "Gabby."

She turned so fast that her curly hair brushed against him. "Oh. Mr. McKay. How are you?"

"Doing okay, for a Yankee." He smiled, hoping she'd see the humor.

Her eyes twinkled as she laughed. "Very good, Mr. McKay. Very good."

"It's Clark, remember?"

"I remember."

The foyer suddenly became very warm, the people very close. He stuck his hands into his pockets. "I was wondering if you'd like to join me for lunch."

She stared at him as if he'd just sprouted a second head.

But then she smiled. "I—I guess." She glanced over her shoulder at the three women forming a semicircle around her. Two of them nodded. A stamp of approval? She faced him again. "That sounds nice."

He offered her his arm. "Shall we?"

She whispered to her friends, then accepted his arm. "Lead the way, McKay."

He glanced to the parking lot, then toward the street. "It's such a lovely day, why don't we walk to the diner? The rental car…well, it's a rental."

"The weather's perfect." Her smile did strange things to his stomach. Like make him forget he'd skipped breakfast after oversleeping. "How'd you like the service? Isn't Pastor Lum the best?"

It was hard to concentrate when she walked so close to him that he could catch whiffs of her perfume. Or shampoo. Something spicy and tangy, not make-your-teeth-hurt sweet. He forced the words past his lips. "I enjoyed his sermon."

"It was good today. The Book of Daniel is my favorite."

"I enjoyed your reading. Very much."

Little dots of pink infused her face. "Thank you." She lowered her lids and stared at the sidewalk.

He'd better change the subject quick or she'd bolt. "Is the diner okay with you?"

Gabby threw her head back and laughed. "It'd better be. It's the only place open for lunch on Sundays."

"Good thing I like the food, then."

"You'd be un-American if you didn't like Ms. Minnie's." She smacked her lips. "That woman can cook."

He chuckled and opened the glass door to the diner. Something about the way she anticipated the food warmed his heart. It was so open and honest. How refreshing.

The diner was packed with locals, all decked out in their Sunday finery. Gabby smiled over her shoulder at him, took his elbow and led him to a booth in the back. They dropped onto the cracked vinyl seats, and Clark glanced around. "Fills up pretty fast."

"After-church crowd is the busiest." Gabby nodded at the waitress who'd shown him so much interest the other night.

She strutted over with a coffeepot and filled Gabby's cup, then smiled at him. "Want a cup, sugah?"

He nodded, keeping his eyes on Gabby, not wanting to encourage the woman.

The waitress poured him a cup of coffee. "Know what y'all want?"

Gabby smiled at the tired-looking woman. Then again, next to Gabby, everyone looked tired, or worn or plain. "I think I'll have the shrimp po-boy, Carol Ann."

The waitress stared at him, popping her gum. "And you?"

"The same."

The waitress sauntered off, stopping at various tables to top off cups.

"Any idea when you'll hear back about your car?"

"I'm hoping tomorrow. Sheriff McGruder asked Lou to rush his report, so I'm anticipating it'll come tomorrow."

"Lou's good. And he's honest." Gabby took another sip, then set down the cup with a gentle thud. "So, tell me about yourself."

"What do you want to know?"

"How old are you?"

"I'm thirty-five."

"Married? Children?"

"No, never married. No children."

"Someone waiting for you back in Philadelphia?"

His heart quickened. Was she interested? In him? "No. I'm all alone."

"Somehow I doubt that." She shifted in her seat.

"What about you?"

She froze. "Me?"

"Yes, you—tell me your life story."

She ran fingers through her hair, shoving it over her shoulder and down her back. "I'm twenty-nine, never married, no children, and you already know I'm a deejay."

"Do you have any brothers or sisters?"

"I have an older brother, Antonio. Luckily, he and Mama and Papa live in Natchez."

"Why is that lucky?"

She laughed. "Let's just say it's lucky for me, so I can live my own life." She flicked her wrist. "What about you? Any brothers or sisters?"

"Nope. Only child."

"How sad."

Clark smiled. "Not really. I was doted on, adored, spoiled."

"Rotten, I'm sure."

"Yeah, I'm sure I was."

"Was?"

The waitress delivering their lunch saved him from answering. As soon as she'd sashayed away, Gabby peered at him. "Would you like me to pray?"

"Yes, please." *And please don't think I'm a heathen for not offering myself, but it's been a long time since I've felt comfortable praying in front of someone.* Even though he'd cleared his name, he'd never forget the way people he thought were his friends had ostracized him. Even the ones who proclaimed to be Christians.

But not Gabby. She flashed another high-wattage smile before bowing her head.

Sitting across the table from her boss was probably the worst idea. Memories of her early times with Blake marched across her mind. He'd been her college boyfriend, and her boss—the station manager at the news channel where she'd interned, back when she was studying broadcast journalism. She'd loved him, trusted him—right up until he'd betrayed her. Handsome, charming, work-focused men couldn't be trusted. Men like Clark. So how could she explain how much she was enjoying lunch with him?

She lifted her sandwich and took a big bite. The zesty Cajun spices set her taste buds on fire, but in a marvelous way. Ms. Minnie did cook like a dream.

Clark mirrored her, and immediately, the air seemed sucked from his lungs. Reaching for his iced tea, he nearly spilled it all over the table. He took a gulp, then another, then another.

She pressed her lips tight together, but her laughter squeezed past. "It's a little hot."

Tears filled his eyes while he drained his tea in a final gulp. Ice clattered against the glass as he set it back on the table.

"Hot?"

He sputtered and coughed.

Gabby had to laugh. His eyes looked like a well-used road map that had gotten wet one too many times. He blinked and blinked—tears ran down his cheeks. The overall appearance filled her heart with giddiness. This was a man she could laugh with. The thought sobered her immediately.

When had Clark slipped under her defenses? The intent way he looked at her? The way he made her feel?

"Hot doesn't begin to describe this stuff. It's lethal." He coughed again. "Man, how do you eat this without smoke coming out of your ears?"

"It's an acquired taste." She smiled as he dabbed the corners of his eyes with a napkin. "The trick is to not take such big bites until your taste buds become accustomed to the spices."

"Gee, that was information you could have passed along a bit earlier."

Ms. Minnie appeared with the pitcher of iced tea. "You okay, Mr. McKay?" she asked as she refilled his glass.

"Just a little spiciness that I'm not used to yet."

The older woman patted his shoulder. "You'll be eating cayenne on your Cheerios after another month here."

His eyes bugged as Ms. Minnie headed to the next table.

"So, I heard you bought a house."

"I did. On Bridges Street."

Her heart and stomach flipped positions. "Do tell."

"A beautiful old antebellum mansion." He swiped his mouth with a napkin. "It's in pretty solid shape, too. I got a good deal."

Gabby let out a sigh of relief. It couldn't be her house—everyone knew the house was priced too high. That was why it had stayed on the market so long. She sat back and allowed herself to relax. Maybe this man wasn't so bad after all.

And just maybe, if she made a good enough impression, her job wouldn't be in jeopardy. If she kept her position, she was almost guaranteed to become syndicated. If that happened, she could afford the down payment and mortgage on her dream home. It wouldn't fix what had happened to Howard or Robert, but at least her life would make sense again.

"So you'll be coming into the station in the morning?"

"Yes. I want to meet with Mr. Masters to discuss some changes."

Personnel changes? Her heart tightened. "Let me know if I can help you with anything."

His smile did strange things to her. "I do have some ideas I want to run by you, but not on your time off."

"I don't mind."

"I appreciate it, but I have a firm policy to not invade on employees' personal time."

Yet, he'd asked her out to lunch. As an employee? For all she knew, he intended to take everyone out to lunch one-on-one to get to know them better. The thought should've reassured her. Sadly, disappointment wormed into her heart.

Gabby took a final sip of her tea, then pushed to her feet. "I really enjoyed lunch, Mr. McKay, but I need to be heading back. I'm expecting company soon."

He stood.

She held up her hand. "No need. I know my way." She forced a smile. "Thank you again. It was a pleasure."

Before he could reply, Gabby spun and marched out of the diner. Her stride quickened as she headed for the church. She trembled. Everything was happening so quickly. The attack. Howard dying. Finding out KLUV had a new owner. Changes.

She turned right on Shannon Street, spying the church's steeple. The tower cut through the skyline. Seemed fitting, some-how—a very visual reminder every day that God lived with people, not merely an omnipresence in some lofty position who didn't care about His children.

Gabby reached her car and started the engine. She took a deep breath. Driving past *her* house would calm her nerves—it always did. She drove toward the residential section of Mystique. Not quite in the city limits, but close enough to be in the town's hub within minutes. A perfect place to have a house. Not only had she been saving her pennies to put down on the place, but she'd been unable to resist some household items she'd found on sale she knew would look beautiful in her home. Excitement built in her chest. As long as she kept her income, she could realistically move into her house in less than six months. Sooner, if her show was syndicated.

If Mr. McKay didn't replace her.

She hung a right on Bridges Street. Gabby perked up in her seat as the house crept into sight. Someone had cut the grass. Strange, since the yard hadn't been mowed in months. Maybe the Realtor had finally gotten around to having it done.

Gabby swallowed a deep breath, her gaze drifting over the top floor of the house. Perfect. As always, the house was perfect. Her scrutiny shifted to the driveway.

She slammed on her brakes. Right in the middle of the street.

The shingle swinging from the bottom of the For Sale sign swayed in the Gulf breeze. The shingle which said, in big, red letters Sold.

She'd barely heard the cell ring. She scrambled to flip it open. "Hello."

"Have you heard the news?" Eric asked.

"What news? I'm not home yet from church and lunch. What're you talking about?"

"Robert."

"He's awake? That's awesome."

"No, he's still unconscious. And if he knows what's good for him, he'll stay that way. If he wakes up, he'll be arrested."

Arrested? She slumped back in her seat. "Whatever for?" Eric had to be wrong. Maybe he'd been listening to Lion Boy's far-fetched alien-abduction theories a little too long, making him daft in the head.

"For Howard's murder."

FIVE

"The sheriff wants to arrest Robert for murder?" That didn't make any sense. "Why would Robert kill Howard? That's just stupid. He was injured in the attack. Knocked unconscious, remember?"

Eric sighed, long and loud. "According to Sheriff McGruder, Robert and Howard fought in public before the murder. The gun that was beside Robert? It's the one that killed Howard. And Robert's prints are on it."

"Has the sheriff gone dotty?" She pinched the bridge of her nose. Hard. This was bad, way bad. Almost as bad as her house having been sold out from under her.

Eric gave a little cough. "You know Howard used to be partial owner of the station, right? Well, the sheriff says Robert bought Howard out a few months ago. I didn't know that. Did you?"

"Y-yeah," Gabby stammered. "I heard something about it at Minnie's a while back."

"This is why I never know what's going on. I don't spend enough time at Minnie's."

"This isn't the time for joking, Eric. What does Robert buying out Howard have to do with anything?"

"Apparently, Howard got upset that Robert was going to sell the station to Mr. McKay. They argued about it. That gives Robert motive."

No. The police had to be wrong. "This is absurd."

"I don't know, Gabby. All I know is they are ready to arrest him as soon as Robert wakes up, which the doctors say is anytime now, and the sheriff will haul him off to the county courthouse."

What was happening to Mystique? She chewed her bottom lip, questions racing through her mind faster than a hurricane in September. "Have you talked to Amber?"

His sharp intake of breath all but hissed against her eardrum. "No. I called first to let you know."

"I appreciate that, Eric. I'll call her."

"Sure thing." He cleared his throat. "I caught Mr. McKay on your show Friday night. Did you know he'd bought the station before he announced it when Howard was murdered?"

"No, I didn't. I mean, I knew Robert was talking about selling, but I didn't know he'd already signed the paperwork."

"Me, either. Well, I need to run."

"Thanks for letting me know." Gabby hung up the phone and stared into space, but didn't focus on anything. How horrible. Robert arrested. Amber would surely be a basket case. Gabby dialed her friend Sheldon's number.

The librarian answered on the first ring. "Hey, Gab. How was lunch with your boss?"

It seemed years ago. "Listen, Shel. The sheriff has decided to charge Robert with Howard's murder." Gabby's mind could barely process what Eric had told her.

"Oh, no! Why?"

"Listen, I'll catch you up to speed on the road. I think we should be with Amber. I'm sure she's devastated."

Devastated was putting it mildly.

"I'll meet you in the parking lot. Rayne's here and will come, too."

"I'll call the others."

* * *

For the millionth time since Clark had returned home from Ms. Minnie's, the image of a sultry dark-haired woman flitted across his mind.

Gabby Rogillio.

Clark slammed the brakes on his thoughts, bringing them to a skidding halt. He clenched his teeth till his jaw ached. This was ludicrous. He was a grown man, experienced in life—there wasn't a single reason why he should feel so drawn to a stranger, a woman he hadn't known existed mere days ago, especially after all his promises to keep his distance from people in Mystique, not get emotionally invested the way he had in Philly. Yet, drawn to her he most certainly was.

The intensity of the attraction was bewildering and…infuriating.

He stood at the kitchen sink, staring out the window into the massive backyard. That so much property came with the house had been a major factor in his decision to buy the house. Now that spring had arrived and the temperatures were balmy, he could divide his time between working on the house and landscaping in the back. He'd spent the better part of yesterday morning mowing the front yard.

Clark couldn't help but feel a sense of joy as he moved around in his new house. It was probably too big for him alone, but something about the old homestead whispered to him.

Calmness. Serenity. Peace.

Things he'd longed for, but that had eluded him.

Not really feeling like working, he plopped down on the couch in the living room and flipped on the television. Might as well get used to the local channels—he didn't have any cable outlets nor did any satellite dish sit on his roof. He'd have to order that soon.

His finger hovered over the remote to change the channel when a newsbreak interrupted the home and garden show. The news grabbed his attention, holding his breath hostage.

Robert Ellison—accused of murder?

Clark stared at the television, his mind blocking out the rambling of the commercial. Mr. Ellison was now the leading suspect in the murder of Howard Alspeed.

The whole situation made Clark uneasy. Robert Ellison hadn't struck him as someone who would commit murder. Especially not at the station. And how had he been knocked unconscious? It'd been obvious he'd hit his head on the stairs, but Clark had assumed the assailant shoved the man, rendering him unconscious, then made his getaway. Probably when Clark and Kevin met at the front door.

This felt wrong in a way that set all his news sensors on high alert. He'd wanted to figure out what was going on, and every instinct he had told him this didn't fit. The sheriff was making a mistake.

But just how much would Clark have to commit to set things right?

As Gabby steered toward the Ellison home, she went through mental excuses. Maybe the sheriff was trying to throw off the real killer in order to trap him. For all that was holy, she prayed that was the case.

"Okay, what's going on?" Immy asked.

"Eric said McGruder announced his intention to arrest Robert. From what we've heard, Robert's prints were found on the gun that killed Howard." She slapped the side of her palm against the steering wheel. "But Robert was a victim himself."

"Just calm down, Gab. It's going to be okay." Immy's voice was calm, steady.

Gabby inhaled deeply, willing the oxygen to soothe the anger roaring inside her, and repeated what Eric had told her. It just wasn't fair. Robert Ellison was a good man, an honest man. A man she loved like a member of her family.

But so was Howard.

She took a right on Shannon Street, passing through the center of town. A gusty March breeze filtered in from the windows lowered about two inches, filling the truck with the promising scent of a spring shower in the very near future.

"I still don't understand. How does McGruder explain Robert's injuries?" Sheldon adjusted the seat belt.

"I haven't a clue." Gabby pressed the brakes as the traffic light turned red at the intersection of McArthur Lane. "Just the fact that Robert and Howard argued isn't enough reason to make him a suspect. At least not to most people." She gripped the steering wheel tighter. "But there's no explanation for how Robert's prints got on the gun."

Robert wouldn't hurt a soul. Not the man who'd hired her right out of college and given her the chance to make a name for herself in the industry.

The Good News Fellowship Church sat on the corner of Shannon and McArthur, nestled among magnolia trees. Gabby stared at the open doors as she waited for the light to turn green. She should call Pastor Lum. He could minister to Amber Ellison. Who knew? Maybe this would be what led the woman back into the fold. Goodness knows Robert had tried hard enough over the years to get his wife to attend church with him.

"That light ain't gonna get any greener, sistah," Tonna said from the backseat, jarring Gabby from her thoughts. Tonna, a woman in constant motion, always thought everyone else should be busy as well. No wonder her hair salon, Tonna's Tresses, was so successful. Then again, she *was* the only salon in town. Still,

Gabby chose to believe it wouldn't matter if there were ten hairdressers inside Mystique's city limits, Tonna's would still be the choice spot.

She pressed the gas, heading into the residential area.

"I still say something's not right with all this." Imogene sliced the air with her hands as she talked. "Robert Ellison's been a member of this community for as long as some of us can remember. There's no way he would do such a thing."

Rayne leaned forward, laying her hand on the center console. "Gabby, you know him better than any of us…could he have done this?"

She didn't know what to believe. She knew what her heart told her—no way would Robert murder anyone, much less someone he considered family—but her mind kept going over the facts of the case. "I really don't believe Robert capable of murder, no matter if he had motive or not."

Conversation halted as Gabby turned into the driveway of the Ellison home. Decades-old magnolia trees lined the long and winding driveway. A wide flower bed trimmed the entire front of the antebellum house, full with greenery of the spring flowers about to burst into full bloom. The lawn appeared lush and well manicured. The hint of wisteria filtered in through the air conditioner. It made a perfect picture, if you didn't know about the tragedy facing those who called it home.

Gabby put the gear in Park and released her seat belt, then let out a long sigh. "Okay, gang, let's go reassure Amber."

God, please let this all be a horrible mistake.

The doorbell chimed the tune of "Dixie" when Gabby pushed the button. The door opened and Amber peered out, her eyes puffy and bloodshot. Gabby instinctively patted the woman's back. "Oh, Amber, I just heard. We're so sorry."

Amber sniffed, then moved to let the girls enter. She pushed the door closed behind them and led them to the sitting room. Imogene wound an arm around Amber's waist and walked with their hostess. Gabby followed, then took a seat on the Queen Anne wingback chair. She stared at Robert's wife sitting on the couch beside Imogene. "Eric called and told me. I'm so sorry. What did the police say?"

More tears and sniffles erupted. Imogene patted Amber's leg. "It's okay. We understand."

Amber smiled politely, but Gabby could tell her heart wasn't in it. "Sheriff McGruder wants to arrest my Robert. Said Robert had murdered Howard." Her voice cracked with sobs. She lifted her gaze to meet Gabby's. "You know he wouldn't do such a thing."

"Of course not." At least she prayed it wasn't so. "I don't understand how the sheriff arrived at such a ridiculous conclusion."

"Well," Amber began, shredding the tissue she clutched, "Robert and Howard argued about the sale of the station. Howard didn't want Robert to sell, but Robert wanted out. And just last week, KLUV lost two big advertisers, making Robert even more desperate." She swallowed, audibly. "But that's Martin Tankersly's fault, not Robert's."

"Martin Tankersly?" Tonna asked from the other side of the room.

Gabby shifted through her mental filing cabinet again. "He owns KROK." The rival radio station, the only other one in Mystique. He'd tried to woo Gabby to his station several times over the past years.

Amber's head bobbed, her brown hair grazing her shoulders. "He undercut advertising prices. The sponsors who went to KROK were the biggest advertisers for Howard's time slot. Sheriff McGruder said that's even more motive for Robert to have killed Howard since he had another year on his contract." Fresh tears slid down her cheeks.

Even though Gabby knew Amber was only forty-seven, with streaked makeup and puffy eyes, the woman looked well into her mid-fifties. Ordinarily, she was an attractive woman. Funny what grief and despair could do to a person. "I didn't know."

"You couldn't have." Amber dabbed her fading brown eyes with the strip of tissue left. "Robert didn't want anyone to know."

"So, the sheriff plans to arrest him?" Tonna inched to the edge of the designer couch.

Amber nodded. "As soon as he wakes up. They have a police guard watching him at the hospital That gun…his fingerprints on it…none of it makes sense to me. Robert's innocent."

"Of course he is," Imogene crooned while patting Amber's shoulder.

Gabby stood and paced.

Amber sobbed harder. Imogene patted her hair. "Don't worry, Ms. Amber, God is with Robert."

Lifting her tear-streaked face, Amber studied Immy. "Do you really believe that? Truly?"

"With all my heart." Immy nodded serenely.

Amber's gaze darted from one girl to the next, who each nodded in agreement. Then Amber stared at her lap. "I hope you're right. All of you," she whispered.

SIX

"All I can say is that Robert Ellison will be charged on counts of second-degree murder as soon as he awakens. That's all I can tell you."

Clark leaned closer as the local news showed Sheriff McGruder on the courthouse stairs. He stared at the television, which only displayed the sheriff's retreating back. The news reporter rambled on, telling the good people of Mystique about the murder of Howard Alspeed and implying no one aside from Mr. Ellison could be guilty. After all, his fingerprints were on the murder weapon.

No comment was made how Mr. Ellison had received his own injuries.

Heat sprinted up the back of Clark's neck. This might be a small town, but the sheriff was wrong in what he was saying, and the news station even more wrong to air his sound bite. Everyone in Mystique watched the news, and most people would believe every single thing said on air. Didn't they realize they tarnished the jury pool with half facts?

Disgust pushing him, Clark shut off the television. Poor Mr. Ellison. Clark knew all about media hype and how what was reported often wasn't the truth. Knew it firsthand and knew it well. He hadn't met Mrs. Ellison, but maybe it would put her mind at ease to know Clark would do what he could to help. He had the Ellisons' home address—maybe he should visit Mrs. Ellison?

Lord, what do I do? I know I haven't been obedient, but I'm trying to get back on track. I could use a little direction here.

Clark paced the worn wooden floors of the living room. Would Mrs. Ellison find him too forward if he showed up on her doorstep at such a trying time? Would it put her mind at ease? He'd have loved for someone, anyone, to have believed in him during his ordeal.

He grabbed his keys and wallet, checked the address for the Ellisons', then headed to his car. Driving into the ritzier part of town, Clark found the house. He parked the car and knocked on the door. No one answered. Had he made a mistake in coming?

Finally the door opened, and a young woman appeared. "Yes? May I help you?"

"I'm Clark McKay. Mrs. Ellison?"

The leggy woman tilted her head. "Uh, no. I'm Sheldon Powers, a friend of Amber's."

"Is Mrs. Ellison here?" He hadn't thought this trip through very well. Mrs. Ellison was probably at the hospital.

"Yes, but I don't think she's up for guests at the moment."

"Shel, who is it?"

No mistaking that voice. Gabby.

She joined Sheldon at the door, displeasure lining her delicate features. "Mr. McKay, what are you doing here?"

"I wanted to see Mrs. Ellison."

"What for?" She planted her hands on her hips, widening her stance. Pure defensive move.

Most definitely he'd made a mistake in coming. Nothing to do about it now. "I just heard the news."

"And what?"

"And wanted to come by and see if I could help."

Gabby's expressive features sharpened. "Help? How can you help?"

He straightened up, amused at how her defensive stance faltered a bit at the reminder of his height. "I thought maybe it would put Mrs. Ellison's mind at ease to know I don't believe Mr. Ellison is guilty."

"What?"

"I realize I don't know him well, but…" How could he admit he knew exactly how Mr. Ellison was feeling?

He paused. "I'd like for KLUV to do a special tonight."

"You've already told everyone you're the owner."

He caught Gabby's eyes narrowing. "I want to come out in support of Mr. Ellison's innocence."

Gabby crossed the threshold, disbelief in her tone. "And you want to go on the air with that tonight?"

"I do. I think our listeners need to know we support Mr. Ellison and—"

A wail broke out behind them.

Sheldon grabbed Gabby's arm, pulling her back into the house. "Mr. McKay, now's really not a good time. Gabby will be at the station on time if you want to discuss further business. Right now, we have a friend who needs us."

Before he could reply, the door was shut in his face.

Surprise gave way to resignation as he made his way back to his car. His idea was a good one, he knew that. But clearly he had more work to do before Gabby or any of the other good people of Mystique truly trusted him.

It occurred to him that he shouldn't care what Gabby thought about him or his motivations. He was her boss.

But he knew better than to lie to himself. What she thought mattered. A lot.

* * *

"Do you think it's possible Sheriff McGruder is right?" Rayne settled into the passenger's seat. Her total logic sometimes annoyed Gabby. This could very well be one of those times.

Gabby started the engine and put the Expedition in Reverse. "I don't know. It's possible, I guess, but I just can't believe it." She glanced at her friend. "What do you think?"

Rayne shrugged. "I just don't know."

Sheldon stuck her head between the two captains' seats. "Logically, I can see where McGruder would come to such a conclusion."

"But we know Robert." Rayne lifted her shoulder.

Gabby's hands tightened on the steering wheel. "I just can't believe this is happening."

"I won't believe Robert's involved," Imogene huffed from the backseat.

Sheldon tapped her fingernails against the armrest. "But his prints on the gun… Maybe he was struggling to get the gun away from the killer before he was knocked out?" Her insight was probably inspired by the suspense novels she read—claiming it was all part of a librarian's duty—but Gabby had to admit that her suggestion made sense.

"Okay, if Robert didn't kill Howard, then who did?" Tonna crossed her arms over her chest.

Wasn't that the loaded question?

Sheldon broke the silence. "I just don't know what to make of it all." She caught Gabby's eye in the rearview mirror. "With Mr. McKay owning the station now, what does this mean for your job, Gab?"

"I really don't know."

Rayne shook her head. "Don't you go worrying about that now, girl. I'll hire you in two shakes of a sheep's tail if something happens."

"Thanks, I really appreciate it." But she wouldn't take that job. No, she hadn't gone to Ole Miss and gotten her degree in communications to work at a bed-and-breakfast, no matter how high in cotton it sat. And she wouldn't leave her field—it'd be like proving to Blake Riggsdale that he'd beaten her. After their disastrous relationship, she'd given up journalism, but wouldn't give up on broadcasting.

"We won't let you lose out on buying that house. We know what it means to you," Immy said in a quiet voice, understanding Gabby's dream.

"Well, when I drove by, there was a Sold sign on it and the grass had been mowed. So, it might not even play into the equation." She let out a sigh that nearly choked her heart.

"Sold?" Immy's eyes widened. "There has to be a mistake. The Realtor swore she'd give you a heads-up if a bid came in on the place."

"I forgot to call the Realtor." Gabby shrugged. "With everything else happening, I guess this will wait."

"Don't worry about things you have no control over." Immy gave Gabby's shoulder a squeeze. "This didn't catch God by surprise. He's still on the throne and still in control."

Gabby couldn't fight the smile tickling her lips. "I know. It's just hard right now to remember that." She parked the SUV in the apartment complex's lot. "Thanks, y'all. I guess I'd better get ready for work. My new boss is coming in. Again." Gabby opened the driver's door and stepped out.

Tonna dug her keys from her purse. "I'll be praying for Robert. And you."

The others echoed their agreement.

"Do we want to meet at Minnie's for supper tomorrow and see where things stand?" Rayne asked Gabby.

"Sure. Seven-thirty?"

"I'll be there," Sheldon stated.

"Me, too," Immy agreed while Tonna nodded.

"Great." Gabby smiled, sending a silent prayer of thanks for having such loyal and loving friends in her life. "I'll call y'all as soon as I can to update."

And she prayed she'd have good news to tell.

Two hours later, Gabby was in the studio. "Thanks for tuning in tonight, Mystique. Tonight we won't be taking calls. Most of you have heard that our former longtime owner, Robert Ellison, was named today as the sheriff department's leading suspect in the murder of Howard Alspeed." Gabby swallowed back the lump in her throat.

Clark smoothly filled the gap her emotions blocked. "I haven't known Mr. Ellison nearly as long as you folks in town, but from what I do know and from the way he conducted the business of selling KLUV, I firmly believe in Mr. Ellison's innocence and am confident the truth will come to light."

She smiled her appreciation. "Thank you for your support, Mr. McKay. Robert Ellison is a pillar of our community, a good man. I stand behind him and will press for the truth to be revealed. The truth about what happened to another member of the KLUV family, Howard Alspeed." Again, emotions held her voice in check.

"Tragedy has fallen on the station, but we believe Mr. Ellison's arrest is just that—a tragedy." Clark straightened, his hands in tight fists on the desk. "We will cooperate with the police in any way possible to clear Mr. Ellison's name."

If she weren't on the air, she might very well have swooned right then. As it was, her stomach did little flips. "I've looked up to Mr. Ellison for years. Some of you know Robert personally, some of you only in passing." Tears clouded her vision. "I won't rest until the truth is revealed, the real murderer is behind bars and Robert's name is fully cleared."

"And I'm authorizing use of the station's resources to assist Gabby in this noble endeavor."

Oh, now she could really kiss him. "So, Mystique, you heard what happened to poor Mr. Alspeed. If you have any information, regardless of how insignificant you may think it is, about the morning of the murder, please call Sheriff McGruder. I'm sure he'll appreciate your help." She queued off her mic, chuckling, and looped a commercial set.

"Bet the sheriff isn't going to be too happy with you."

"No, I doubt it." She shrugged. "But maybe, just maybe, somebody will have seen a car or something. We've gotta help where we can because McGruder sure isn't looking any further for suspects than Robert."

"Oftentimes, truth is the first casualty when an investigation begins."

She detected something in his voice. Sadness? Gabby narrowed her eyes, studying him. "Speaking from experience?"

"Well…"

She held up a finger. "Hold that thought for just a second." Gabby leaned over her mic. "Instead of taking calls tonight, I'll be playing some songs from Robert's and Howard's favorites list. To remember and honor these members of the KLUV family." She flipped off her mic and queued up a music loop.

Leaning back in her chair, she gazed at Mr. McKay. "You were saying?"

He held that thought…and saw no reason to volunteer the information about his past. The smear campaign that had been waged against his paper, the friends he'd lost when he'd refused to back down from the truthful, if controversial, article—all of that was part of his past he'd be just as happy to forget.

The bitter taste of betrayal still scorched his tongue.

Gabby cleared her throat, still waiting for a response.

"Nothing."

He looked at Gabby, the studio light highlighting the nostalgic tears in her eyes and the soft smile on her face.

Yes, he was more than willing to forget the past when the present and future seemed so bright.

SEVEN

Coffee was a little bit of heaven on earth.

Gabby sniffed deeply, then savored the strong flavor. Nothing started her day like coffee. Especially when her day started earlier than normal. But sleep had eluded her after her show, teasing her until she'd finally fallen into a restless slumber.

Until ten-thirty.

Unheard of for her to be up at such an hour after working until six. But something had jerked her from her fragmented dream state. So she sat at the kitchen table sipping coffee, about to read the morning paper. She took another sip of coffee and unfolded the newsprint.

Her heart clutched as she read the headline.

Former Radio Station Owner Accused of Murdering Employee.

The coffee soured in her stomach as Gabby read the article, which went on to imply there was a divorce looming for the Ellisons, putting a dark slant on the argument between Robert and Howard in Ms. Minnie's café and casting suspicion upon the recent sale of KLUV to Mr. McKay.

How dare the reporter print such unfounded claims? "According to a source close to Robert and Amber Ellison, a divorce sits on the horizon." What kind of hogwash was that? She'd just seen Amber, who hadn't even hinted at an impending divorce.

And Robert hadn't indicated anything of the sort. Talk about unethical reporting.

"Robert Ellison and Howard Alspeed argued publicly about the sale of KLUV, multiple eyewitnesses claim." Gabby tightened her grip on the newsprint. It crinkled in response. Even the mildest of disagreements in the café would sound like a war after the gossips finished their tale. "Multiple witnesses"—Gabby had learned back in college that eyewitness accounts were the most unreliable. How irresponsible of the reporter, not to mention the editor, to give them such credence.

And that the article all but implied Robert had murdered Howard because they'd argued about Mr. McKay buying the station. That was just ludicrous.

Even worse, the article cited the forensic evidence. Like Robert's fingerprints on the gun left at the scene. The gun that ballistics affirmed had been used to fire the killing shot. How had Robert's fingerprints gotten on the firearm? Was Sheldon right—could he have wrestled with the killer for the gun?

But the evidence also posed more questions. If Robert shot Howard, how did Robert get hurt? The newspaper article implied he and Howard had struggled for the gun, and after Robert shot Howard, he fell backward, hitting his head and knocking him unconscious. Gabby couldn't buy that. While both men were physically fit for their age, Howard was clearly the stronger man.

What, exactly, had really happened?

Gabby slung the newspaper across the kitchen table and shoved to her feet. She'd get to the truth. She'd prove Robert innocent. And then she'd take the reporter, and his editor, to task for such sloppy reporting.

She gathered her purse and headed to the grocery store. Maybe if she got enough pints of ice cream, it'd cool her temper.

Then again, maybe not.

Steaming mad, Gabby stormed through her grocery shopping with the force of a class-4 hurricane, hoping her friends and neighbors who she passed as she shopped would have the good sense to keep their distance. For the most part, they did. Right up until she sped around a standing display of Tony Chachere's and smacked right into Clark McKay.

"I take it you read the article," Clark said.

Gabby's face turned a brighter shade of red and the muscles in her jaw twitched and jumped. "It's disgraceful. The paper all but convicted him without even waiting to hear his side!"

He bet she didn't have a clue how cute she was when flustered. Clark studied the flames flickering in her eyes. Probably wouldn't be the smartest move to comment on that Gabbyism right now. "One thing I'm curious about. They mentioned Mr. Ellison's fingerprints on the gun. I've heard nothing about if they found gunpowder residue on his hand."

She snorted—a subtle, ladylike snort, but a snort just the same. "You know, they probably didn't even check." Her head jerked right, then left, her gaze scanning the aisle. "Or they did and didn't find any. I wonder if they let his attorney know."

"So Amber's hired an attorney even though the charges haven't officially been filed?"

"They'll be as soon as he wakes up. Why wait? But the lawyer—he's nice and all, but I don't know how well he'll do. Honestly, I don't think there's ever been a murder in Mystique. At least not one that went to trial."

"So he's not familiar with criminal defense?"

"No."

Clark let out a long, tired sigh. "That doesn't bode very well for Mr. Ellison. Is there anyone else we could hire? The station would pay for his legal fees."

Her beautiful eyes widened, and he thought he caught a glimpse of respect and gratitude shimmering in the irises. "It's a kind offer, but there's no one else here."

There it was again—the challenge in not only her words, but her eyes, as well. That look made him want to be the man he thought he'd left behind. The man who fought the battles that needed fighting, no matter what the odds. "Then we'll have to help."

That stopped her in her tracks. Those expressive eyes of hers widened. Her hands dropped from her hips and hung loosely at her sides. She shifted her weight from one heeled foot to the other. "You really *do* believe he's innocent."

"I do. And I meant what I said—we'll use all of KLUV's resources to uncover the truth. Mr. Ellison might have already sold the station when Mr. Alspeed was murdered, but Mr. Alspeed was an employee. I want to get to the bottom of this."

"Me, too. Where do we start?"

"Let me do some digging and see if I can find out about the gunpowder residue. That'd be a good starting point."

Her mouth dropped open, hung agape for a long second, then her lips clamped shut. "I need to get these groceries home."

"Why don't I meet you at the station when you're done? We can put together a game plan of sorts." He held his breath, then argued against his own logic. Why did he care a flip what she thought? She was an employee. He was her boss.

"I'll finish up here, then meet you at KLUV. Eric should be there now. Talk with him. He's been station manager for several years. Even though he's a little young and cocky, he seems to have a good head on his shoulders."

Except she wasn't aware of his conversation with Eric, where the station manager had all but told him to back out of buying KLUV. What would she say if she knew?

Turning away from him, she headed to the registers, her step still brisk and purposeful, but thankfully no longer as anger-fueled as it had been.

Clark watched her go, questioning himself. Just why, he railed against his stupid emotions, did it matter so much what opinion Gabby Rogillio had of him? He couldn't answer.

He only knew it did.

After completing his shopping, checking out, then running the staples to his house, he headed to KLUV. He whipped into the parking lot, taking note that Gabby's SUV was already parked in its familiar place.

He strode into the coolness, grateful to be out of the early afternoon's unforgiving sun.

"Hello, Mr. McKay." The part-time receptionist, Ellen, smiled a little too brightly as she stood and handed him several slips of paper. "Here are your messages. I'm glad you got here before I left so I could give them to you personally."

"Thank you." He gave her a curt nod and took the slips. He'd have to see about hiring an afternoon receptionist soon. "Are Eric and Gabby in his office?"

"Yes, sir." She grabbed her purse and slung it over her shoulder. "With the door closed," she whispered.

What did that mean? What was she implying? Maybe he'd just hire someone else as a full-time receptionist.

He didn't bother to reply, just strode down the hall to the station manager's office. The door wasn't closed, not really. There was a crack. He tapped on the door. It swung open.

Gabby sat in the chair in front of Eric's desk. Both bolted to their feet, but neither looked uncomfortable at his interruption. His heart thudded a little faster.

"Would you like to go to your office?" Gabby asked.

"No. This is fine." He took the other seat in front of Eric's desk, and Gabby sat back in her chair.

Eric sat, as well. "I spoke with Kevin. He's covering Howard's time slot for the time being."

"Thank you." Clark noticed the bead of sweat on the station manager's upper lip. "We'll need to consider hiring someone on a permanent basis for the position."

"We usually run an ad in the Natchez paper." Eric glanced at Gabby, then tiptoed his gaze back to Clark. "Unless there's someone you already have in mind."

Ah, so that's why the station manager was so nervous—worried he'd be firing people to replace them with his own crew. Maybe this was what had prompted Eric's little talk with him before.

Clark smiled and leaned forward, resting his hands on the desk. "I have no one else in mind." He cleared his throat. "Let me go ahead and get this straight—I have no intention of clearing house to bring in my people."

Eric smiled. "That's a relief."

"I mean it. I don't want to disrupt a good team." He curled his palms into fists. "Now, we will have to hire someone to take over the morning slot. I'd prefer to hire locally if at all possible."

"I'll get an ad together and get it in the paper." Eric nodded.

Clark cut his eyes to Gabby, who sat stiff, staring at the undecorated wall. What was going through that quick mind of hers? "Gabby, your thoughts?"

She jerked her attention to him. "Me? Why ask me? I'm just a deejay."

"The best one this station has, according to the numbers. I'm asking your opinion."

Her cheeks tinged pink. "Then I agree with what Eric suggests. Ads. Interviews. Whatever." She flicked her wrist and waggled her fingers.

"But we're a team, and I want to make sure everyone gets along. Can't have feuding." As soon as the words left his mouth, Clark wished he could pull them back. Feuding…that's what put Robert Ellison in the sheriff's crosshairs for murdering Howard.

Gabby's eyes bugged and moistened, pushing Clark's regret even further.

He swallowed against a dry mouth. "I'm sorry. I didn't mean to imply—"

She shook her head. "No reason to apologize. I get what you're saying. I do." She blinked furiously. "It's just hard."

"I know." His own voice thickened.

"How about I run the ad and do preliminary interviewing, then when there are only a few good candidates, I bring them in to interview with you, Mr. McKay, and you can introduce them to any of the staff? Would that work?" Eric held a pen over a pad of paper.

"Yes. Thank you."

Gabby smiled at the station manager. "Eric, you rock."

Clark's breathing hitched.

What would it take for Gabby to think *he* rocked?

EIGHT

The gossips had beaten them to supper—their gums already flapped about Robert's situation.

Gabby led Clark through the packed crowd at Ms. Minnie's, weaving her way to the table where the rest of the girls sat. The peppery-spicy aroma of crawfish bisque permeated the diner, making Gabby's stomach growl. She dropped into the chair beside Rayne and pulled Clark beside her.

His nearness did strange things to her, but she fought against the attraction. His willingness to help clear Robert made her feel things she had no business feeling.

Sheldon tapped her flawlessly manicured nails against the table. "Okay, bring us up to speed. All the talk in the library this afternoon was about the article. I've heard all the rumors floating around. What's the truth?"

"Actually, Tonna," Gabby said, "I need to know all the dirt you've heard about Robert and Amber Ellison's marriage."

Perfectly tweezed brows arched as Tonna leaned over the table. "I thought you didn't like grapevine gossip."

"This is important." Gabby's stomach knotted at the thought of actually asking for hearsay on her boss. Yet, with everything the article had said…

Clark cleared his throat.

"Jump in, Mr. McKay. We're all here to help and Gabby told us on the phone that you're with us. So speak freely." Rayne flicked her hair over her shoulder.

He smiled and focused on Tonna. "It seems likely the Ellisons were heading for divorce."

"Well," Tonna leaned against the cheap vinyl covering the back of the chair, "since y'all asked…rumor has it that Robert thought Amber's been steppin' out on him. For years. And he ain't none too happy about it." She gave a curt nod to emphasize her point. "And talk today implied she was seen with Howard on more than one occasion."

Sheldon shook her head, loosening a few strawberry-blond tendrils from her librarian bun. "Well, shut my mouth! People really think Amber was having an affair with Howard? I just can't see it."

Tonna shrugged. "I'm only repeating what I hear, sistah. Mary Sue was just a-gabbin' about it to Ms. LouAnn not even a month ago in the shop."

"And they really think there was something between Amber and Howard?" Gabby traced the grooves in the tabletop with her fingernail.

"Oh, great day in the morning, Gab, you can't believe that ole biddy Mary Sue." Imogene shifted in her seat to face Gabby. "Come on, what gives? Why do you even care what the Geritol set is talking about?" She stirred her iced tea. "What does Amber have to say about all of this?"

"She isn't saying much. In fact, she's barely talking at all." Gabby replied. "Just crying."

"I don't want to believe it, either." Rayne lifted a shoulder. "But with all the rumors, I have to wonder."

Gabby bit her bottom lip, praying the tears wouldn't come. "But most of all in this whole travesty, I just think Robert's innocent."

"Of course you do, honey. He's treated you like a father ever since he hired you." Sheldon tore open two sugar packets from the dispenser and dumped the contents into her iced tea. "We all know how much you think of him."

"It's not just that. It's… I don't even know how to explain it. It's just a feeling I've got. In my gut."

"Sure that ain't hunger rumbling about?" Tonna laughed. Carol Ann hoisted a tray of bowls over their heads. Gabby smiled at the waitress whose eyes were weighted down with wrinkles.

"How's your momma and them, Rayne?" Carol Ann asked as she set steaming bowls of bisque in front of them.

"They're fine, Carol Ann."

The woman sashayed away from the booth, hollering out greetings as she passed tables.

Imogene bowed her head, and the other girls followed suit. After the blessing, the shaker of cayenne pepper made its way around the table before Gabby spoke what drummed in her heart. "We aim to find out the truth."

A cloak of silence fell over the table as everyone ate.

Finally, Clark's gaze collided with Gabby's. Chills fingered up her spine as he dipped his head. "We *will* find out the truth."

Gratitude gripped Gabby's heart in a tight squeeze. She peeked at her watch, then finished off her iced tea. "I gotta run, or I'll be late to work."

Clark eased to standing and offered his hand to Gabby.

She took it and straightened. Her heart beat erratically. "I'll call y'all tomorrow. Keep an ear out for anything about Amber or Robert, okay?" She turned and rushed to the door, thankful for the excuse of work to make a fast getaway.

The man made her feel things, think things… Well, she didn't want to analyze everything now.

As she cranked the engine of her vehicle, Gabby hit the speed-dial number of her cell phone for the Realtor's office. She glanced at the clock. Yeah, they'd probably left for the day, but she'd leave a message.

"Mystique Realty." Wow, they were still there.

"May I speak to Margaret Worth, please?"

"Just a moment."

Elevator music filled her ear, annoying her further. Why couldn't the local businesses support the radio station and pipe in KLUV's broadcast?

"This is Margaret. May I help you?"

"Hi, Margaret, it's Gabby."

An uncomfortable pause echoed against Gabby's eardrum. "Oh. Hi, Gabby." Another long beat of silence. "I guess you heard the house sold."

"I did." Gabby's hand shook as she tried to steer and clutch the cell phone at the same time. "I thought we had an understanding you would give me some warning when a bid was placed on the house."

"I'm sorry, Gabby. Really. It all happened so fast. He just moved to town, needed a house fast. That one was vacant and ready to move into."

"I see." But she didn't. Oh, her head understood the good fortune of the realty company, but her heart screamed at the betrayal.

"I'm really sorry. Mr. McKay had cash for the asking price, so there was no delay in the processing. I didn't have time to call you."

Mr. McKay? So he had bought her house.

"He's such a nice man."

A nice man? He'd done moved into *her* house. She knew she wasn't exactly being fair—it's not as if he'd known—but it was hard to remember to be reasonable.

"Thanks, Margaret." She snapped the phone shut, not wanting to hear any more apologies or platitudes.

Gabby slammed the side of her fist against the steering wheel. What an awful thing to find out about Clark McKay. And just when she was starting to like him, too.

Her breath caught. Starting to… She hadn't really thought she was starting to like him, had she? Mercy. Maybe this news had come at just the right time. Liking Clark McKay was the last thing she wanted to do.

"Good thing you didn't drive it back on Friday night. The brake line was cut."

Clark stood in the garage, staring at Lou, hearing his words, but not wanting to accept them. "Someone deliberately cut my brake line?"

"No question, Mr. McKay." He held up the damaged part. "See here, it's jagged and diagonal. Means somebody did it quick. From the part cut, looks like it was accessed by the tire well. You must not have had your tires straight, had to have been turned a little when you parked. Gave somebody easy access. Guess they figured if you didn't heed that warning, they'd make sure you'd have no choice but to speed right on out of town."

Someone wanted to hurt him. "Have you told the sheriff?"

"I did. He wants me to send this over to him as soon as possible." Lou waved the cut line. "I'll have Fred drop it by the station this evening."

Who would want to hurt him?

"But the good news is, your car is fixed and ready to go, new paint job and all."

"Thanks, Lou. I really appreciate you getting right on this." Who would do this to him? Why? "Here's a question for you—how long ago do you think the line was cut? I mean, did it have to have just happened before I had the accident?"

Lou punched in Clark's invoice in the cash register. "Not necessarily. Depending how often you've driven it and how often you've used the brakes, it could've happened several days before the accident."

Someone could've done it before Howard's murder. This could be not even slightly connected to his owning KLUV. But who? Why?

Then again, it could've happened since, which made more sense.

Clark handed over his credit card and waited for Lou to complete the transaction. But his mind spun.

Howard—once a part owner of the station, shot dead. Robert—previous owner of the station, knocked unconscious and left for dead, providing Clark didn't believe he'd shot Howard. Now him, his car—new owner of the station, someone tampering with his brakes to cause him harm.

Clark scrawled his name at the bottom of the charge slip. Three men, all owners or very previous owners of KLUV, all victims of senseless, violent attacks.

He took his keys, turned over the rental's and strode to his car.

Who wanted KLUV owners out of the way? And what would they try next?

Time to be proactive, not reactive.

Gabby parked her SUV in KLUV's parking lot and headed to the building she'd called her second home for years. Eric's car still sat out front. She checked her watch again. He must be working late.

The welcome blast of cool air slammed against her face as she entered the station. With sure steps muffled by the industrial-grade carpet, she headed to the studio. She stopped outside Eric's office and peered inside the open door.

He hunched over the computer keyboard, his fingers flying as the *tap-tap-tapping* filled the room, subdued only by the sounds of the station's broadcast filtering through the speakers. She cleared her throat, and he jerked upright.

"Is it that late already?" He jabbed his hand through his hair.

"Yeah. I'm on in fifteen." Gabby crossed the office to linger in front of his desk. "Whatcha doing?"

Eric let out a long sigh. "Trying to figure out the financial status of the station for Mr. McKay. Remember, he asked some payroll questions." He waved toward the computer.

Just what she didn't want to hear.

It wasn't that she didn't care about the station's finances—of course she wanted the station to do well—but the desire to uncover what was really happening at KLUV drove her harder. Truth be told, not knowing the truth nearly sucked the life right out of her.

"I don't believe Robert killed Howard." Gabby perched on the edge of the desk. "I won't believe that."

"Who else could it be?" Eric laced his fingers behind his head and leaned back in the chair. He suddenly appeared much older than his twenty-nine years. "Who would do this?"

Gabby shrugged. "I don't know, but I intend to find out."

His palms dropped to the desk with a thump as he sat straight. "You know, I heard you and Mr. McKay on the air, vowing to support Robert. Shouldn't finding the truth be left to the police?"

"Sure, if they're willing to actually look. In this case, they aren't." Gabby swung her leg slowly. Back and forth.

"Do you think that's wise? I mean, making the commitment to look into things. If, as you say, Robert isn't the murderer, then you might be putting yourself in the hot seat."

She hadn't thought about that. "I'm just trying to figure out who had a beef with Robert and Howard." She snapped her fingers. "You know, Amber said something about Martin Tankersly undercutting his advertising prices."

"Please. My stepfather's a jerk, no doubt about it, but I don't think he'd do something like this." Eric shrugged. "He's tried to get Howard to come to work for him over the years, but Howard never would. I can't see Martin doing something so desperate now."

"You're his family, right?"

"Family?" He grunted. "You must be kidding. He hated me from the day he married my mother. After she died, he knocked me around quite a bit when I was growing up." He steepled his hands over the desk, anger glimmering in his dark orbs. "Didn't you wonder why I came to work at KLUV instead of going to work for him?"

"I guess I never thought about it." She should have. Eric working for his stepdad's rival could only mean they'd had a falling out. A serious one. Would Mr. Tankersly be mad enough to exact revenge? But why Howard and not Robert? Why now? And how did someone tampering with Mr. McKay's car fit into this?

"He's scum of the earth, I'll attest to that. He's got some serious anger issues. But why would he do something like this? Doesn't make sense."

"Well, I think it bears looking into." Gabby shifted to stand. "I'm going to look into every possibility."

"I understand where you're coming from, Gabby, I do." Eric shook his head, his eyes downcast. "But you might want to prepare yourself for the possibility that Robert *is* guilty."

"I won't accept that."

"Think about it. We all knew how strongly Howard felt about the station. And he had another year on his contract. But then Robert decides to up and sell the station. To an outsider."

Gabby didn't like the path Eric was on, but she had to admit that everything he said was true.

"They were heard arguing about the sale." Eric crossed his arms over his chest. "Maybe the argument went too far and Howard refused to let it go. Robert knew he'd already signed the papers with Mr. McKay. What else could he do but shut up Howard?"

"I won't believe that." Gabby shoved away the creepy phantom spiders crawling up her spine and glanced at her watch. "Time for me to hit the airwaves."

"I'll just be a little longer." He frowned.

Gabby nodded and turned toward the studio. She grabbed her call sheet and slipped inside just as David Gray, the evening deejay, signed off his segment. David patted her shoulder as he passed, obviously anxious to get home to his wife and kids. Gabby flashed him a smile before dropping into the leather chair.

Settling into the studio, she queued up her microphone. "Good evening, Mystique, this is Gabby Rogillio. Call now and give me the dedications of your heart. I'm waiting to hear from you."

If only she could find a way to ease the burdens of *her* heart.

NINE

Clark tucked himself into the sports car and headed home. It'd been a long day, starting with the meeting with Gabby and KLUV's station manager, and ending with Gabby and her friends. Tomorrow would be another long day.

Spinning his car onto his street, Clark let out a tired sigh. The streetlights flickered as he crept along the residential area, the moon playing hide-and-seek behind the low-lying clouds. The sweet fragrance of magnolia blossoms and some other blooming flowers filled the air. On the radio, KLUV's announcer had read the latest news.

As he turned the car into the driveway, a sultry voice spilled from the speakers. Clark turned up the volume.

"…so call me, Mystique, and give me the dedications of your heart. This is Gabby, and I'm waiting to hear from you."

A soft love ballad came over the airwaves, jarring Clark from his trance. He coasted the car into his garage. It took all of five steps to enter into the kitchen. Forgoing the television, Clark lifted the remote for the stereo and clicked it on, seeking for KLUV's frequency. The same song filled the living room.

He slumped onto his leather couch, welcoming the comfort. He didn't bother to turn on a light. Closing his eyes, he waited until the last notes of the song faded out.

"I have a special dedication for Rich, going out tonight from Allison. She wants you to know that she loves you with all her heart. Love is in the air tonight, Mystique. This is for you, Rich and Allison. Love well." Gabby's throaty voice drifted to a whisper as the opening chords of "Reunited" played.

The vision of her face danced across his memory, tugging at his heart. What was the woman doing to him? Hadn't he come to Mystique to hide, to regroup, to take control of his life again? And now some little Southern belle had his emotions wound up tighter than a spring, even more than the media killer he'd escaped.

He crossed the room to the kitchen, jerked open the refrigerator and pulled out a soft drink. The cold liquid quenched his thirst, but not his desire to see Gabby, talk to her, hear her voice all to himself. Clark set the bottle on the counter with a thump, then stomped back into the living room.

"...that's right, call me. Tell me what's in your heart tonight. I'm waiting to listen."

Man, but the woman's voice did strange things to him. Made his knees feel like Jell-O.

Father God, what's happening to me?

When he opened his eyes, that's when he noticed the broken patio door.

His heart jumped into his throat. He lifted his cell phone and dialed the sheriff's number, walking through the house as he did. Finding nothing amiss on the bottom floor, he headed for the stairs.

The dispatcher answered the phone, then put him on hold for McGruder.

He opened the door to his bedroom and froze.

Someone had trashed his bedroom.

Less than thirty minutes later, Sheriff McGruder spoke to his deputies, then returned to the living room and faced Clark.

"They're dusting for prints now. Did you notice if anything was missing?"

"In that mess? I couldn't tell." Why would someone break into his home and trash his bedroom, of all places? "My computer and stereo equipment are all downstairs and they weren't taken."

The sheriff harrumphed and wrote more in his notebook. "You know, Mr. McKay, I have to wonder."

"What?"

"With your cut brake line and now this…well, I'm wondering if someone's got something personal against you."

You think? Clark cleared his throat, determined not to let the lawman get a rise out of him. "I would assume so, Sheriff."

"Seems strange that these things happened right after you bought KLUV."

"Yes, it does."

"Any ideas about the correlation?"

Clark couldn't stop the retort burning his tongue. "If I had an idea about that, don't you think I'd say something to you? I really don't like my life being in danger, nor my house being trashed."

"Mmm-hmm." McGruder shut his notebook and shoved it into his pocket. "I'll file my report. The guys should be finished here in a few minutes. If you notice anything missing when you start cleaning up, let me know and I'll add it to my report."

"That's it?" Clark bolted to his feet.

"What else would you like me to do, Mr. McKay? We're dusting for prints. We've inspected the crime scene, we're making a report. What more can we do?"

How about find out who's behind it? Clark gritted his teeth. "When can I pick up a copy of the report?"

"Tomorrow after ten."

"Thank you."

"I'll see myself out." The sheriff headed to the front door, paused, then turned back to Clark. "You know, if I were you, I'd be very careful. Seems to me there's at least one person who isn't exactly thrilled with you being in Mystique."

Before the sheriff could leave, he was approached by a deputy with a piece of paper in his hands. "Sir, we found this upstairs."

McGruder donned gloves, unfolded the paper and stared at it for a long moment, long past the point where Clark started to get impatient.

"What is it?"

"See for yourself." The sheriff held up the page for Clark to see.

In bold, black letters it read LEAVE NOW OR YOU WON'T BE THE ONLY ONE TO GET HURT.

Clark's heart jumped into his throat. This was hardly the first threat he'd ever gotten, but this one scared him like none other had, because now he wasn't the only one at risk.

Gabby.

The sun crested over Mystique, pushing through the front blinds at KLUV. Gabby nodded as David pointed toward the break room and answered the phone. "KLUV, this is Gabby."

"Gabby, this is Clark."

"Hi." Her voice sounded funny. "What's up?"

"My house was broken into tonight."

"What? When? How?"

"As far as we can tell, nothing was taken. They broke into the patio door, but they didn't bother anything downstairs. Just trashed my bedroom."

"That's awful. I'm so sorry." But now there had been two separate attacks on Mr. McKay. There had to be a connection between these events and the assault on Howard and Robert.

"I just wanted to let you know." He paused, and she got the

feeling he was trying to decide how much to tell her. "Um, has there been anything unusual happening at the station?"

"No, it's been quiet all night." She stifled a yawn. "And David just made it in."

"Well, okay then. Just…keep an eye out when you leave the building. Rest well and I'll talk to you this afternoon."

"You take care, Clark." She hung up the phone as David entered the studio with a steaming cup of coffee.

She smiled, gathered her things and exited the station. Gabby shoved her sunglasses on the bridge of her nose. She made her way to her vehicle, glancing onto the street, and pressed the button on her remote. The doors unlocked with a click.

Gabby reached for the door handle and noticed a piece of paper lodged under the windshield wiper. She groaned as she opened the door and tossed her purse in the passenger's seat. People knew better than to put sale ads or solicitations on vehicles. She stood on the running board and snatched the paper off. She'd call and complain to whomever the paper promoted. Her heart raced as she read.

BACK OFF.

Gabby swallowed hard. Back off of what? Was this some kind of joke? She eased to the pavement, gripping the paper tightly, shut the driver's door and leaned against the Expedition. Was this meant for her personally? She took off her glasses and squinted in the harsh sunlight, looking around the parking lot. If it was a joke, someone would be around. Only David's car sat in the lot, a row over.

What to make of it? Her sense of equilibrium wavered, and she leaned against the vehicle once again.

A car whipped into the back lot. Gabby spun around. Kevin parked and nodded at her. "Sorry I'm late. Traffic." He ambled toward her. "Man, what happened to your tires?"

She swallowed back the lashing she had at the ready for him and glanced at her front tire. Flat as a board. She looked at the back tire—flat, as well. On shaky legs, she circled the vehicle. Her mouth went slack. All four tires were flat.

Kevin kneeled by the driver's tire. "Looks like someone slit them." He stood and peered at her. "Who'd you tick off?"

Kevin might find amusement in this vandalism, but Gabby sure didn't. She glared at the news reporter. "I need to call the sheriff."

"Yeah." He trailed her to the front door of the station. "Wonder who would've cut your tires."

Gabby ignored him and reached for her cell in her purse. She dialed the sheriff's number.

"McGruder."

"Sheriff, it's Gabby. My tires have been slashed."

"Where?"

"At the station."

"I'm on my way. Don't touch anything." The sheriff disconnected the call with an echoing click.

Gabby shut her cell. The man needed to seriously work on his manners. She stared at the paper still wadded in her hand.

Right on the heels of the attack on Clark's house. What did it all mean?

The police scanner crackled to life.

Clark jumped—he must've dozed off until the scanner woke him. He'd almost forgotten it was on, it'd been so quiet. He stood and moved to the scanner.

Just as his hand hovered over the on/off button, the report came through. Vandalism on a car at KLUV. He waited for additional information, holding his breath. Finally, the dispatcher told him what he wanted to know—Gabby Rogillio had reported the incident.

Without further thought, Clark grabbed his keys and headed out the door. He drove to the station, his mind racing. He had to make sure Gabby was okay.

He turned into the parking lot, relieved to see the sheriff had already arrived. He parked and headed toward Gabby's SUV. Didn't have to wonder about the act of vandalism—her tires were slashed.

"What are you doing here?" Gabby's eyes were tired.

"Heard you might need a ride home." He deliberately put a teasing tone in his voice. Despite her false bravado, he could see how upset she was.

"How'd you hear about this?" the sheriff asked.

"Police scanner."

"You listen to a police scanner?" Suspicion edged into her voice.

"Old habit."

She turned back to the sheriff. "I think the note shows someone doesn't want anyone looking into Howard's murder. Or are you going to claim Robert did this, while unconscious and under guard?"

What note?

Sheriff McGruder shook his head. "Doesn't mean anything, Gabby. I doubt it has anything to do with Howard's murder."

"But it clearly reads Back Off." She stabbed a finger at the piece of paper in the sheriff's hand. "What else could it mean?"

Someone sent her a letter telling her to back off?

"I don't know what it means, but I'm pretty sure it has nothing to do with Howard or Robert." The sheriff shifted his weight from one foot to the other. "Heard there's talk of your show being syndicated. Maybe that's what the letter means."

Clark took a deep breath. He had yet to discuss the possible syndication with Gabby. Of course she was well aware that her show was under consideration, but Clark hadn't had a chance to speak with her over details. The interest of syndication had been one of Robert's strong selling points.

Her face turned red. "I don't think so. It has to do with me looking into Howard's murder. Someone's warning me to stop."

The sheriff's face twisted into a grimace. "I don't believe that. Why don't you just let us handle this, Ms. Rogillio? It's safer all around if you don't start sticking your nose where it doesn't belong."

Gabby went rigid. "I believe this threat on me has made it very much my business, Sheriff."

The tension built. Clark moved beside Gabby. "But you'll process the letter for any evidence, right, Sheriff?"

Gabby cut her eyes at him, relief glittering in the orbs.

The sheriff glared at him. "Of course, I'll process the letter. I know how to do my job, Mr. McKay." He jotted something on a small piece of notebook paper and passed it to Gabby. "You can pick up a copy of my report tomorrow after one. You'll need it to file a claim with your insurance company."

Right before Clark's eyes, Gabby wilted. He stuck a hand under her elbow. "I'll give you a ride home. I'll pick you up tomorrow afternoon and take you to the sheriff's office to get the report. You'll need to go ahead and call your insurance company to file the claim."

She blinked several times, and Clark wondered if maybe she didn't hear him.

"Oh, and you can't move your truck yet." The sheriff cast a scathing glance at Clark, but spoke to Gabby. "We need to *process* it for evidence."

That snagged her attention. "What am I supposed to do for transportation?"

"Guess you'll have to rent a car." McGruder shrugged and ambled toward his cruiser.

No empathy at all in the man. Clark didn't understand

McGruder's rudeness. "Your insurance might provide a rental for you."

Gabby sighed. Her shoulders drooped as if she would swoon. But Gabby Rogillio wasn't the swooning type of woman. She'd just been hit with a lot, all at once.

Clark eased his hand under her elbow. "Come on, I'll take you home. You can call your insurance company."

Without argument, Gabby let him lead her to his car. She slipped into the seat, her eyes wide and fixed. After he'd started the engine, he shifted to face her. "Um, where do you live?"

She rattled off the name of the apartments over on Sea Swept Lane. He put the car in gear, all the while kicking himself. With the murder and the tampering of his brakes, he should've upped security at the station. Now there was vandalism at his house and at the station. He made a mental note to call a security company today and procure some surveillance.

"I can't believe McGruder doesn't get the connection." Her tone jerked Clark from his thoughts.

He cut his gaze over to her. "What connection?"

Coloring drifted back into her face. "That letter and Howard's murder. Back Off is pretty clear to me that I'm on the right track in refusing to believe Robert murdered Howard."

"The letter said Back Off?" He fought to concentrate on his driving.

"Yep. They left it under my wiper. And slashed all my tires. That's a message I'm on the right track." She gripped the strap of her purse. "And I intend to find out what someone's trying to stop me from learning."

She would put herself in danger. What had the sheriff been thinking, goading her like that? And had Clark contributed by going on air with her and pledging his support to Robert? Surely Gabby understood the difference between encouraging people to turn evidence over to the police and actively seeking out a killer. Clark cleared his throat as he turned onto Sea Swept. "Maybe you should let the police handle the investigation, Gabby."

She jerked to face him. "Are you kidding me? Sheriff McGruder doesn't even think this is connected. The jerk."

"Well, he might have a point." Clark wanted to swallow back his reply as soon as he saw her expression.

"What?" Gabby shook her head. "That's the most asinine thing I've ever heard. What kind of man *are* you?"

Ice ran through Clark's blood as he whipped into the apartment complex. "Which way?" He held the steering wheel in a death grip.

She nodded toward the back of the complex. "If you believe that note has nothing to do with Howard's murder and my looking into it, then you really *are* a dumb Yankee."

"Guess everyone's entitled to their own opinion." Clark brought the car to a halt and hit the button to unlock the doors.

She opened the door, her eyes narrowing. "I suppose so. Thanks for the ride home."

"Would you like me to take you to the station tomorrow to pick up your report?"

"No." She stood on the pavement of the parking lot. Her arms trembled as she got her footing. "I'll find my own way, thank you very much." She slammed the door before he could say anything more.

Although he could pinch her head off right now, he waited until she'd climbed the outer stairs to the second-story landing and moved from his line of sight before he spun out of the parking lot.

As soon as he got home, though, and saw his broken patio door, his mood changed. He was worried about Gabby's safety, that's why he'd wanted her to step back from investigating, but

Gabby didn't see it like that. She'd promised to help her friend and to her way of thinking, that meant doing everything in her power to clear Robert's name. Normally, he'd admire such loyalty…if he wasn't so worried about her putting herself in danger. And how had Gabby felt? He'd backed her before in her support of Robert. She must feel he'd abandoned her now. No wonder she'd lashed out.

He could feel guilt rising inside him. He shouldn't have argued with her. Shouldn't have let his own feelings lead his words. He'd have to figure out a way to apologize to her.

Properly.

TEN

Buzz!

Gabby rolled over and batted her hand around the nightstand. She made contact with the alarm clock, hit it again for good measure, then buried herself back under the covers.

Buzz! Buzz! Buzz!

She bolted upright, knocking the pillow to the floor. Gabby teased her fingers through her hair, her mind staggering to shove aside the cobwebs of sleep, the dreams of intense hazel eyes with amazing gold flecks mingling with the memories of Blake's deception. She shook her head. Hadn't she just silenced the alarm? She cut her eyes to the clock—ten o'clock, and yep, it was most assuredly off.

Buzzzzzzzzzz!

Oh, good gravy, it was the doorbell. If it was the rental car representative again, she'd scream. It'd taken the better part of two hours to file her insurance claim and arrange to have a rental delivered this morning. But she'd stressed they were to drop off the car and leave the keys under the floor mat. If they were waking her up to give her the keys…

Gabby shoved off the bed, and immediately fell to her knees. The soft down comforter twisted around her legs. "Hang on, I'm coming." After untangling herself, she tottered to the living room and peered through the peephole.

A huge bouquet of white roses filled her line of vision. Surprise squeezed her chest. Flowers? She'd been woken for someone who didn't even have the right apartment? Nothing like starting her day with such luck.

She flipped the dead bolt and whipped open the door, just as the delivery man's finger punched toward the buzzer again. Gabby stiffened. "Can I help you?"

"Uh, yeah. Delivery for...a..." He stared at the white envelope hanging from the vase. "A Ms. Gabby Rogillio." His eyes darted back to hers. "That you?"

"Y-yes." That squeeze tightened a notch as she held out her hands for the vase. She almost lost her grip as she took it, the weight unexpectedly heavy. "Thank you."

Kicking the door closed behind her, Gabby carried the arrangement to the glass dinette table and set the vase in the middle. She leaned over and inhaled deeply, the back of the padded chair digging into her abdomen. Sweetness infiltrated her senses, and she smiled. Her fingers caressed a single silky petal as she mentally counted the buds. Twenty-three...twenty-four. Two dozen Confederate roses. Wow.

She carefully pried the card from the envelope, her heart colliding with her stomach.

A Southern rose for a Southern flower. Clark McKay

Her heart did a somersault while she pressed her lips together, her gaze drifting from the roses to the card. The man knew how to make a statement, she'd give him that much. She took another deep breath over the flowers. The subtle fragrance tickled her nose. Not too shabby for a Yankee.

With a trembling hand, she laid the card on the table and leaned her shoulder against the doorway, staring at the flowers. They were beautiful. Very beautiful. It was thoughtful of him to have sent them. When was the last time she'd gotten flowers, roses nonetheless, from a man? Her high school prom? Her sorority days? She couldn't even remember. Certainly not ever from Blake.

She might just have gone off half-cocked on Clark this morning. When had her life gotten so complicated?

Brring!

Gabby jumped at the phone's ring. She grabbed the cordless from the kitchen. "Hello."

"I thought you might be awake." Imogene's smooth voice slid across the phone line and over Gabby's tormented mind.

"Hey. How'd you know?"

"Something just told me to call you. So is everything okay?" Immy's voice cracked with concern. "Did you sleep okay? I'd have had nightmares if I'd received such a threatening letter."

"No, I slept just fine."

"So, what's not right?"

Gabby smiled. How like her friend to be so in sync with the hearts of others.

"Aww, Immy. I think I may have made a harsh judgment against someone." The confession, once it passed her lips, eased Gabby's conscience just a tad. She slipped into one of the cushy dinette chairs and stared at the flowers.

"What'd you do?" No condemnation, no discrimination, just love and sympathy in Immy's sweet voice.

She recounted the horrible way she'd snapped at Clark this morning. After ending with the delivery of the flowers, Gabby held her breath.

A long silence loomed. Then finally, Immy's full chuckle

erupted. "Oh my stars, Gabby, that man's sure got your feathers ruffled, doesn't he?"

"This isn't funny," Gabby said, but the corners of her mouth tickled as she fought to keep the smile out of her voice.

Immy's laughter screeched to a halt. "No, it's not. You owe him an apology."

"What?" Sure, she might have acted hastily in word and deed, but apologize? Gabby touched the edge of a rose petal. The smoothness caressed her back.

"You were rude to him, unfounded I might add, and he's made this big gesture toward you. You owe him an apology."

"I'm not so sure about that. He bought my house, Immy. My house." Gabby took a sip of her café au lait, then set the mug on the table. Her gaze locked on the card lying on the table, and the coffee soured in the pit of her stomach.

"Oh, Gab, I'm so sorry, hon. But there's no way he could've known."

"But Immy…" She knew she whined, but couldn't stop the overflow of emotions.

"Come on, Gab, it isn't his fault Howard was murdered and Robert arrested. He had his car vandalized and his house broken into." A heavy pause hovered through the connection. "Sweetie, he's not Blake Riggsdale, you know."

"So you keep reminding me. But I think he *is* keeping things from me, like Blake did." Gabby ran a finger around the lip of the mug. The pain of Blake's actions still hurt, even though it'd been years since he'd used her.

"He's only known you a couple of days," Immy said. "Give him time to open up. And such a big gesture with the roses. Great day in the morning, Gabby, are you blind? The man's totally smitten with you, and you're giving him the brush-off. You're acting like a silly little nitwit."

"Yeah, the roses were a nice touch. But I can't help wondering why."

"No man can know the heart of another, Gabby. Only God can. And He's also the only one in a position to sit and pass judgment." She let out a loud sigh.

Now Gabby's stomach really roiled. The bile of self-condemnation inched up the back of her throat. She pressed her lips together tightly, then swallowed. A lump stuck in her craw. Her gaze focused on the roses again.

Immy's voice softened. "I'm not saying that to make you feel guilty or bad, but to make you see what you're doing. You don't know why Mr. McKay's sending you flowers. But you can't just assume to know. That's not your place."

"I know," Gabby squeaked out. Her heart jumped. "You're right. I need to call him and apologize."

"That's my girl." Immy chuckled. "Don't beat yourself up over this. God knows you're under enough stress and you're just trying to help Robert. You just need to make sure you don't hurt other people in your crusade." A long pause followed. Then, "And that he bought your house, however unwittingly, probably added to your annoyance with him."

Boy, had she ever hit the nail on the head with that one. "Thanks, Immy."

"No worries. I've got to run. I need to go check on Mr. Tobias. His Alzheimer's is getting worse."

"Oh my. I'll say a prayer for him."

"Thanks."

Gabby stared at the dead phone in her hand. She should call Clark, her heart reverberated Immy's words.

No, she needed to do more than that. She had to go to Clark to talk. This apology deserved to be made in person.

* * *

Had she received the flowers yet? Clark opened another spreadsheet on his laptop.

Uneasiness nestled tight in his chest. Gabby seemed positive of Robert's innocence and if she was going to put herself in danger by investigating, he was going to help. How else could he protect her? Besides, having been a journalist for years, Clark agreed something didn't seem right. Oh, he believed the Ellison marriage was in trouble—that much he'd detected. Poor Robert. He was a deacon in the church—a divorce wouldn't sit well with the elders, especially in a small town. But a murderer? No, Clark was with Gabby on this one—he couldn't believe Mr. Ellison was a cold-blooded killer.

A knock rapped on his front door, startling him. He hadn't had a single visitor aside from Aunt Beulah. Who'd be coming now?

Clark shoved to his feet and swung the door wide-open. His heart fell to his toes.

Gabby stood on the threshold, looking better and fresher than any woman had a right to. "Hi, Clark."

"Hi."

"I wanted to thank you for the roses. They're lovely."

An in-person thank-you. That had to be good news, right? "You're most welcome. Would you like to come in?"

"Um." She hesitated, her gaze dropping to the floor. "I need to apologize to you, as well."

"Whatever for?"

"I was rude. I'm sorry."

Her honesty was his undoing. "Then we're both forgiven?"

"I guess we are."

"Would you like a tour of the house?"

Darkness passed over her expressions. "I can't." Were those tears forming in her eyes?

Maybe she knew the previous owners and was sad they were gone. The reason didn't matter. He needed to get back on the even footing from a moment ago. "Let's prove there are no hard feelings between us. Bury the hatchet once and for all."

"How's that?" Her eyes widened, suspicion dancing in their depths.

"Have dinner with me. Tonight."

"Supper. Your Yankee tendencies are showing."

"Excuse me?" Would his place of birth and raising always be a punch line to her?

"In the South, we refer to the night meal as supper, not dinner."

"Supper, then."

"I work the nightshift at the station, remember? I go on at ten."

He chuckled. "I'm not likely to forget. Could we maybe eat before you have to go to work?"

"I—I guess so. Do you want to meet at Ms. Minnie's?"

"Actually, I was thinking more along the lines of Sam's Steakhouse."

Her lips pursed as she debated. Finally, she let out a breath. "What time would you like to meet?"

"Why don't I pick you up at eight? I'll make reservations."

Gabby grinned. "You don't need reservations at Sam's on a Tuesday."

"Oh. Is eight good for you?"

"Sounds fine." She moved toward the door.

"I'll pick you up then."

Her voice cracked. "Uh, Clark?"

"Yeah?"

"Thank you again for the flowers."

Gabby pulled the rental car into the VanDoren Bed & Breakfast parking lot and killed the engine. She stared through the windshield at the valets milling around their outpost, not really sure what she was doing. Why'd she come here?

Because Rayne was her most fashionable friend and, in spite of herself, she really wanted to look nice for Clark.

She headed to the front entrance. People moved about the grand foyer area. Lots of people. Way too many for this time of year. Was Rayne hosting some kind of event? Guilt that she'd been so wrapped up in her own issues and emotions lately that she hadn't even thought to inquire about her friends' lives pushed her toward the front desk.

"Hi, Gabby. Here to see Ms. VanDoren?" the young girl behind the counter asked.

Gabby couldn't even remember her name. "Yes. Is she in?"

"Go on back."

She headed down the hall and paused outside of Rayne's office. The door sat ajar, and she could detect Rayne's I'm-not-pleased-with-you tone in her voice.

Gabby ducked her head inside. Rayne sat at her desk, looking like a dark-blonde Barbie doll propped in a massive leather chair behind an oversize desk. The phone stuck against her ear, Rayne spied Gabby and waved her in. Gabby dropped into one of the three Queen Anne chairs facing the desk as Rayne wrapped up her call.

Rayne hung up the phone and studied Gabby's face. "So, what brings you by?"

She couldn't even voice her concerns. "Nothing. Just wanted to drop by and see how you were. How the B and B is doing."

Rayne's smile lit up the dark-paneled room. The office didn't suit her—it was too dark, too masculine. No wonder, her father had designed it for himself. "We're holding our own. Right now, we've only got two vacancies." Her excitement showed in her eyes.

"That's great." She hoped Rayne hadn't picked up on the cracking of her voice.

Rayne studied her a bit more intently. "But that's not the real reason you came by. What's up?"

Busted. "Uh, I was wondering if you could suggest something for me to wear tonight."

"Tonight? Where to?" Rayne's eyebrow shot up.

"Clark's taking me to Sam's Steakhouse for supper."

"Oh my. I didn't know."

"He just asked me today."

Rayne moved to sit on the edge of the desk, her legs dangling in front of Gabby's. "Today? Do tell."

Gabby explained about the letter, the slit tires and Clark being a rock during the stressful time. "He sent me flowers." She smiled, and heat fanned her face.

"Flowers? Really." Rayne crossed her arms over her chest. "What kind of flowers?"

Gabby swallowed. "White Confederate roses."

"Oh, I see."

"It's just supper."

Rayne laughed. "Sure it is. And white roses, excuse me, white Confederate roses, too."

"Okay, okay. It's a date. A real-live-I'll-pick-you-up date." Gabby snorted. "Happy now?"

"Happy for you." Rayne moved to peer out the floor-to-ceiling window. "Let's see, Sam's Steakhouse. Hmm."

"It's just a restaurant, you know."

"How about that black dress you wore to the Cotillion?" Rayne faced her.

Gabby shook her head. "Lost three buttons and haven't had a chance to get replacements."

"The red dress with the gold piping?"

"Long sleeves. I wore it at Christmas, remember?"

"That's right." Rayne paused for a moment, then snapped her fingers. "The purple sundress?"

Possibly. "You don't think it's too casual?"

"For a spring supper? Nah. It's just a restaurant, you know."

They both burst into laughter.

"Then the purple sundress it is." Gabby gave her friend a hug. "Thanks. You're the best."

"Yeah, yeah, yeah. Just don't you ever forget it."

As if Gabby could.

Rayne hopped off the edge of the desk. "Go home and get ready for your date with Clark. Enjoy your evening."

Gabby stood and forced a smile. "I'll try."

"Remember what Ms. Minnie always says…triers never do."

"And doers never try," Gabby finished.

Rayne touched her hand. "Gab, are you okay?"

Emotions threatened to hold her words hostage. Gabby nodded.

"Seriously?"

"I'm fine. Just have a lot on my mind about Robert and Howard."

Rayne's penetrating stare pinned her to the spot. "I'm sure that's part of it, but I think there's more."

"Do tell?"

"I think you're really attracted to Clark McKay."

Heat flooded her face and Gabby ducked her head. "Don't be silly. We just happen to be on the same side of an issue."

"Gabriella Rogillio, stop it right now. Why can't you just admit you like Clark?" Rayne crossed her arms over her chest.

Tears blurred Gabby's vision as the floodgates to her emotions broke free. "Because what if he turns out to be just like Blake? I can't go through that kind of betrayal again." A trail of tears slipped from her eyes. "I couldn't survive the pain."

"Oh, Gab." Rayne pulled her into a hug, holding her tight. "You can't let that jerk Blake ruin your chances for happiness."

Gabby stepped out of the comforting hug.

"It's okay to be scared. Be scared silly. Love can be a scary thing." Rayne wagged a finger. "But don't let that fear stop you from being happy."

"Love? Not hardly." But the idea slipped into the recesses of her heart. What would it feel like to really love someone, and be loved?

"You mean, not yet." Rayne smiled. "Let down your guard and see where it leads."

At that moment, her intercom buzzed. "Ms. VanDoren, a guest would like to see you for a moment."

"I have to go, but think about what I said. Tear down those silly walls you've built up. Get to know Clark's heart. He just might surprise you."

He already did. A hundred times over.

ELEVEN

Clark stared out the window, absently studying the magnolia trees swaying in the early evening breeze across the street. Dusk settled over Mystique. A sweet fragrance drifted on the wind, swirling through the open space and filling his house.

Thank You, Lord, for showing me I needed to get away. For giving me such an enormous wake-up call.

He'd noticed things sure were slower down in the South—the people, the business, the way everyone talked, the entire town seemed to live by a slower pace.

Clark glanced at his watch—seven-twenty. Just forty more minutes until he could leave to pick up Gabby for their date. He'd already showered, shaved and dressed, but needed to cool his heels. He refused to be early for their date.

Wasn't timing everything?

In the corporate world, timing *was* everything. But here, in sleepy little Mystique, and with his heart…was timing important?

Sad, but he had nothing to compare his emotions to. No woman had ever made him break out in cold sweats before. Not like Gabby did, effortlessly.

Clark tossed the pen onto the desk and let his thoughts drift. Eventually, he glanced at his watch again—seven-forty. He grabbed his suit jacket from the coatrack, slung it over his shoulder and rushed out the door into the humid evening. While he didn't want to be early, it wouldn't do for him to be late.

He drove toward her apartment, stopping at a red light. He glanced over at the florist shop on the corner. If the delivered roses had made an impression, what would one more being hand-delivered mean? When the light turned green, Clark jerked his car into the florist's parking lot.

The clerk called out a greeting as the little bell over the door twinkled, then her eyes widened when she recognized him. Her hands stilled at the arrangement in front of her. "Mr. McKay. Were the roses satisfactory?"

"Perfectly."

The relief showed in the woman's smile. "Good. Good." She wiped her hands on her green apron. "What else may I help you with?"

"Do you happen to have a single red rose?"

She laughed. "We're a florist—of course I have red roses. What kind?"

"Do you have a red Confederate rose?"

"I believe I do." She moved toward the refrigerator case. "Would you like it in a vase, with greenery?"

He closed his eyes and conjured up Gabby's image. "No, just the rose wrapped in paper, please."

Why did Murphy's Law always have to apply? The phone rang when Gabby was in the bathroom.

She hopped from the shower in a cloud of steam, wrapped the fluffy terry-cloth robe around her and then scrambled to the bedroom. Her wet feet lost traction and she slipped, slamming her knee against the nightstand and knocking the phone off the hook. "Ouch."

Breathless, she grabbed the receiver and pressed it to her ear. "Hello."

"Did I interrupt something, sistah?" Tonna's laughing words held a hint of mischievousness.

"Yeah, my shower. I fell and bumped my knee, and it's all your fault." Gabby giggled as she perched on the edge of the mattress, rubbing her tender kneecap. "What's up?"

"Oh, sorry 'bout that. Listen, girl, you won't believe what I just heard."

"Tonna, you know how I feel about gossip." Gabby plucked a loose thread from the robe and let it drift to the floor.

"I thought you said you wanted me to keep my ears open about Robert." Her tone came out sounding hurt.

"Oh. Right. Okay."

Tonna's laugh rumbled from her throat. "I love ya, you little hypocrite."

That stung, even if said in jest. "It's for the greater good, Tonna." At least she believed that. *Lord, please help me keep my motives pure.*

"I know, honey. I'm just joshin' with ya anyway. So, Ms. LouAnn and Ms. Roberta were in the shop this morning, getting dye jobs. Can you imagine someone wanting their hair to look burgundy? I declare, I think when senility sets in a lack of taste creeps over your common sense."

"Ton-na."

"Oh, yeah. Sorry. Anyways, the two ladies had breakfast over at Ms. Minnie's this morning—sat across from Sam Wood. And lo and behold, guess what his favorite topic of the morning was?"

"Robert?"

"Bingo!" Tonna lowered her voice. "According to Ms. LouAnn, Sam Wood slapped down the morning paper, his face all in smiles, and said, 'Serves him right.' Then, as Ms.

Roberta tells it, Ms. Minnie asked Sam what had stuck in his craw so early in the morning. And Sam tells her, loud as can be, so Ms. LouAnn says, that he's glad Robert Ellison's gonna be behind bars and hopes he rots there until his dyin' day. Can you believe?"

"Oh my." Gabby didn't know Sam Wood very well, but it had been obvious for years that there was no love lost between him and Robert. She'd never wondered why before, just blew it off as none of her business. Maybe she should have asked a couple of questions. "What else did you hear?"

"Well, Ms. Roberta says Ms. Minnie went into her lecture about not wishing ill of anyone, but says that Sam just guffawed at her—can you imagine anyone guffawing at Ms. Minnie?—and said, and I quote, 'Robert deserves every ounce of hardship he gets.'"

Sam's dislike of Robert ran so deep that he'd be happy about another's misfortune? "What else?"

"Ms. LouAnn says Ms. Minnie 'bout had a tizzy right there in the middle of the diner. Said she pulled out that handkerchief from her dress, dabbed at her forehead, then put those hands on her hips and told Sam Wood that she wouldn't tolerate any bad lip about any of the citizens of Mystique and if he couldn't keep civil, he could go somewhere else for his coffee."

"Oh, my soul and body. Not a good idea to tick off Ms. Minnie."

"Ms. Roberta says Ms. Minnie's admonishment didn't matter a lick to ol' Sam. He just gave a big belly laugh, tossed some bills on the table and sauntered out as nice as you please."

What was happening to their town? Mystique hadn't seen this much excitement since LindaMae had lost her Ms. Mystique title after being found rolling around in the hay with Bubba behind the church. "My, my, my. Anything else?"

"Nope. Ms. LouAnn and Ms. Roberta finished their coffee and headed over this way." Tonna took in a deep breath. "What do you think of all that, Gab? Could Mr. Sam have something to do with Howard's murder?"

"I don't know, but I'll look into it." Gabby ran a hand through her wet and matted hair. Everything about the situation was getting curiouser and curiouser, as Alice would say.

"I gotta go. My next client is here."

"Thanks, Tonna."

Gabby rolled over the conversation in her mind. Ms. LouAnn and Ms. Roberta might have misheard some of that conversation, but probably not much. Well into their late sixties, neither of them was hard of hearing, nor were there any black holes bumping around in their brains. So why did Sam Wood have such a beef with Robert?

More importantly, did it have anything to do with Howard's murder?

She rushed through putting on makeup and getting dressed, still pondering what Tonna had told her. Nothing made sense. Gabby struggled to secure her long hair back with pins, just as the doorbell buzzed. Her hair won the battle.

Her heart went aflutter as she grabbed her purse. This was silly, to be such a nervous ninny. She'd had plenty of dates and none of them caused her to spin into such a dither. Then again, none of them had been with Clark McKay.

She tossed a glance in the mirror. Not too bad. The purple sundress was not only flattering to her coloring and shape, but wore quite comfortably. She needed to be at ease in her clothes.

Buzz!

"Just a minute," she hollered into the hall as she jerked up a tube and spread the color shine across her lips. She blotted twice, dabbed the edges, then rushed to the front door. Gabby stopped with her hand on the knob, took in a deep breath and then pulled the door open.

Her heart did a triple backflip. She fought for air.

Clark McKay was a vision of suaveness, pure and simple. His dark hair with gray strands just beginning to streak out at the temples was cut short enough that the evening breeze didn't muss his style. He wore a loose pair of khaki pants and a plain button-down cream shirt, which just enhanced his strong build. And then there were his eyes—those intense, gold-flecked eyes, lined with such lush lashes that all the girls had probably hated him growing up—even now, a stab of jealousy ripped through Gabby over the feature. He peered down at her with such intensity, heat spread up the back of her neck.

"You look lovely," he breathed against her as he leaned forward and planted a soft, feathery kiss on her temple.

Funny how her headache evaporated in a snap as his lips teased her forehead.

Her heart went *pitter-patter, pitter-patter* before she gave herself a mental shake. "Thank you." She lifted her gaze to his and grabbed her purse from the foyer table. "You look downright dashing yourself." She reined in her traitorous heart.

"This is for you." He handed her a rose in green paper. A single red rose. A Confederate rose.

She took it, holding it to her nose and inhaling deeply. My, but the man sure had a way about him. A way of washing in under her defenses. "Thank you." She pulled it from its wrapping and stuck it in the middle of the arrangement of white roses on the dinette table. Right in the center. It looked perfect.

He glanced around. "You have a nice place here."

"Thank you." But the knot in her stomach tightened. Not as nice as *her* house. The one he'd bought. No, it wasn't his fault. He didn't know. But the little imp sitting on her shoulder asked if he had known, would it have made any difference?

"Shouldn't we be going?" Gabby asked, slipping her purse's strap over her shoulder and striding toward the door.

His light touch at her elbow sent sparklers off inside her. She smiled as she pulled the door closed and let him lead her down the stairs to his car.

What a car. It wasn't merely an automobile, it was…an entity. A pristine, cherry-red convertible Mercedes-Benz. The old style SL600, not those new little coupe numbers. Wow, what a ride. How'd she miss noticing when he'd driven her home?

"Where'd you get this?"

"This is my pride and joy." Clark hesitated. "Do you like it?"

"Like it? What's not to like? I love it." She rushed forward, inspecting the beauty and running her hand lovingly down the hood. The metal was still warm from Clark's drive over. "Sweet."

His deep chuckle caused her to stare at him. "What?"

He shook his head. "I've just never known a woman who appreciates cars as much as you obviously do."

Heat fanned up the back of her neck and marched across her face. She ducked her head and mumbled, "My older brother's into cars."

Clark laid his arm across her shoulders. The warmth seeped through the cotton material of his shirt, making her nerves tingle. She glanced at him, the butterflies doing aerobics in her midsection.

"I like a woman who can appreciate a fine vehicle." Those tawny specks sparkled in his eyes, and the air froze in her lungs.

"Shall we go?"

Gabby nodded. Her tongue seemed glued to the roof of her mouth all of a sudden. She slipped into the warm leather seat, then locked her seat belt after he shut the door with a gentle thump. When he turned over the engine, a blast of cool air splayed across her face. She leaned toward the vents, praying the coolness would equalize her fair and telling complexion. The fresh scent of leather and coolant tickled her senses.

"How was your day?" he asked.

She pressed her lips together. How was her day? At least it wasn't as bad as discussing the weather. "It was just a normal day." Well, normal except for Tonna's tidbit about Sam Wood. She filled him in.

"I don't know him. Maybe I can ask Aunt Beulah if she knows anything."

"That'd be helpful. I just can't figure out what's happening here." He smiled. "We'll figure it out."

"Anything interesting happen with you?"

"Nothing." Clark cleared his throat. "Nice weather today, huh?"

The abrupt shift of topic caught her off guard. She burst out laughing. He obviously was desperate for topics of conversation.

His eyes darted from the road to her face. "What?" He looked like some poor little puppy left abandoned on the side of the road.

The giggles kept coming. The confusion swimming in his eyes was her final undoing. Her giggles made way for the fit of laughter bubbling in her chest. Gabby held her stomach and bent over, but it was a losing battle—she laughed so hard tears spilled from her eyes and she cackled.

"Gabby, are you okay?"

She held up a hand and fought to compose herself. The nervousness worked its way into the giggle fit, and it took all of her self-control to stop her outburst. Just when she thought she had her chuckles aptly managed, she glanced at him. At the sight of his sincere, concerned expression, she lost her tenuous hold on her control again, doubling over and shaking with laughter.

"Gabby?"

"Oh, C-Clark." She straightened and bit down on her bottom lip as she faced him. "Th-th-the…w-weather?"

The corners of his mouth shot up, then the car filled with

his booming laughter. The two of them chuckled until he whipped the little sports car into the lot of Sam's Steakhouse and parked.

"Milady," he said as he opened her car door and bent into a low bow.

"Thank you kindly, sir." She curtseyed and laughed again. Oh, it was so nice to be with a man and just laugh at life, revel in the silliness. Blake had never laughed with her—at her, maybe, but never with her and certainly never at his own expense.

Once seated at a window table, they perused the menus the waiter placed in their hands before whipping away to fetch their drinks. The restaurant had small round tables covered in white linen cloths. Each setting boasted a single candle in the center of the table, surrounded by greenery. The candlelight cast a romantic ambience over the room.

Clark's gaze met hers over the leather-bound menu. "What's good here?"

"The steak, of course." She let her eyes scan down the menu. "The fried shrimp is good, too. Oh, and the jambalaya is to die for." Gabby let out a soft sigh and closed the menu, already tasting the spicy rice and chicken entrée. "That's what I'm going to have."

"If it's that good, then I'll have it, as well." He laid his menu down atop hers, and took her hand in his. "Now, tell me everything there is to know about Gabby Rogillio."

How could she think when his thumb caressed her knuckles? She licked her lips. "Um, I thought we'd already covered all these bases."

"There's more to you than just those facts." He leaned forward, his eyes hypnotizing her. "Tell me why you love cars."

Good. Safe subject. "My brother, Antonio, loves refurbishing classics." She shrugged. "Growing up, he always had a heap of junk, as Mama called them, parked in the yard. Always planning on fixing them up and selling them." Her lips curled up at the memories. "I guess it rubbed off on me a little."

The waiter appeared with a basket of bread and their drinks. Gabby pulled her hand back into her lap as Clark gave their orders. She reached for a piece of bread and lifted the butter knife. "What about you?"

He slipped her an easy smile. "What about me?"

"Tell me about your life before Mystique." She took a bite of the warm bread, savoring the yeasty taste.

Clark blinked, then his eyes stayed in a wide, caught-in-headlights kind of look. "Not much to tell."

Why the panic flashing across his face like a neon sign? He stared into her eyes. "I think I'm going to love being in Mystique, though."

The bread felt like lead in her stomach. "How do you like your new house?" The words nearly choked her. She should tell him it was her dream house. She should, but it was too close to her heart. Too personal. How could she share with him when he wouldn't open up with her? She took a deep breath and remembered her talk with Immy. Maybe he just needed more time.

"The place needs some minor repairs and updating, but I'm looking forward to the work."

"It's a beautiful place." She blinked back the stinging tears.

"I'd love for you to see what I'm doing with it. I want to restore it to its full, original glory."

Words wouldn't form. She shoved another piece of bread into her mouth and nodded.

Didn't he see this was ripping her heart out? "Sure." Was she stupid?

The waiter stopped by their table, took their order, refilled their drink glasses, then faded into the background.

"Are you and your brother close?"

She took a sip. "We are. I love Antonio, don't get me wrong, but it's nice to be out from under his watchful eyes."

"A bit overprotective?"

Gabby laughed. "He's an Italian big brother—what do you think?"

"So, it might be a good thing he's not here. Now." His eyes turned serious.

If she didn't blink, she'd swear she could see her future in his shiny orbs. She swallowed, then reached for her glass. Frissons of fear mingled with excitement spidered up her spine.

"I didn't mean to make you uncomfortable." His voice hitched.

No, but he did. Only because her emotions were as traitorous as Benedict Arnold.

Before Clark could say any more, Sheriff McGruder ambled up alongside their table. Gabby let out a silent sigh. Couldn't she just enjoy a nice evening with a gentleman without someone intruding?

"Gabby. Mr. McKay," the sheriff interrupted with a nod to each of them. "Sorry to disturb you."

Clark made a movement of pushing back his chair.

"Don't bother to get up, Mr. McKay," Sheriff McGruder said in his gruff voice as he gestured for Clark to remain seated. "I just had a question I needed to ask you."

Leaning back into his chair, Clark ran a hand over his chin. "Okay."

The sheriff jammed his thumb through his belt loop. "When we uncovered the note yesterday threatening you and—" he looked over at Gabby "—someone else, why didn't you tell me about the threats made on your life back in Philadelphia? That you were told they'd get you—no matter where you ran."

Gabby's throat tightened. Someone had threatened him and *her?* Why hadn't he said anything? Surely he wouldn't keep something like that from her. McGruder had to be mistaken.

There was no mistake. Clark's expression, with hooded eyes and guilty flushing, told her there wasn't any mistake. He looked like…like…Blake. Her heart slithered to her toes as she pushed to her feet. Her chair tilted precariously for a moment, then toppled backward to the plush burgundy carpeting.

Clark shoved to his feet, as well.

"Don't bother," she snapped with all the iciness she could muster into her voice. With knees that threatened to give way, Gabby turned and stomped determinedly out the door of the restaurant.

The salt-filled breeze kissed her face, but she ignored it. This could be the key to finding the killer, yet all Gabby could think of was that Clark hadn't trusted her enough to tell her the truth. Something fishy was going on here, and it had nothing to do with the Gulf nestled several hundred yards away.

Gabby didn't know exactly what was going on, but as long as there was breath left in her body, she intended to find out.

If only her heart didn't shatter at the realization that another man she'd started to care for had betrayed her trust.

Just like Blake.

TWELVE

The dagger of betrayal Gabby's eyes had shoved into Clark's heart twisted as she rushed away. He moved to follow her, but the sheriff laid a hand on his shoulder.

"Best let her cool off a bit."

Clark slumped into his chair and raked his hand across his face. What must Gabby think of him now? The date had been going so well, too. Disappointment coiled in the pit of his stomach.

"So, you gonna answer my question?"

"What?" He jerked his head up and focused on the arrogant lawman still hovering beside the table.

"Why didn't you tell me about the threats?"

"The police in Philly found them to be without intent. Nothing ever happened, so the threats must've been just that—threats." Clark shrugged. "But I'm guessing you've already talked to the police and already know all this."

"Uh-huh." Sheriff McGruder shifted his weight, his battered cowboy boots scuffing the polished floor. "But didn't you think you should've mentioned it?"

"I guess. Honestly, I didn't see a connection."

"Even after your brakes were cut? Your house trashed? Don't make a lick of sense to me."

"I'm not you," Clark ground out, then pressed his lips together. No reason to alienate the local authorities, even if the sheriff did reek of small-town inadequacies. "Look, to be honest, I didn't even think about the threats. They were in reaction to a controversial story my paper covered, trying to scare me off. It didn't work. Why would the people who threatened me then choose to act *now* when they didn't follow through on their threats at the time?"

"Those threats the reason you ran away from the big city?"

Nosy, that's what the man was. Yet, Clark couldn't afford to not be open and honest. Already his lack of being forthright had turned Gabby against him. "Not exactly." How could he explain the betrayal he felt? "After I ran a controversial story, some people turned against me, tried to destroy my credibility. I eventually cleared my name and the reputation of my paper. But some of the people who smeared me were supposedly my friends, my supporters…well, when they jumped on the bandwagon against me, I—"

"Ah." Sheriff McGruder gave a knowing nod. "Yep, that'll make you hightail it for parts unknown for sure." He clapped Clark on the shoulder. "I'll see you around."

"Yes." Great, so the sheriff understood. But how could he explain things to Gabby? His breath hitched.

God, what can I do to make this right?

I'm just eat up with stupidity.

Gabby stumbled from the restaurant parking lot, blinking back angry tears. Why hadn't she trusted her gut instincts to be leery of Clark? A Yankee up and moving to Mystique should have made her keep her distance. Her intuition had all but written in the sky that Clark was just like Blake. Had she just wanted to be deceived? Had she played right into Clark's hand?

Gravel in the parking lot crunched as her steps punctuated her emotions. She turned onto Sea Swept Lane, marching toward her apartment complex. One of the best things about living in such a small town was that nearly everything existed in walking distance.

A gentle breeze danced along the street, the thick aroma of the Gulf wafting through town. The tears wouldn't be denied any longer, springing from her eyes and streaking down her face. The wind dried them on her cheek.

How could she have been so blind, so led astray by a handsome stranger's charm? She'd allowed herself to be swayed by Clark's intense eyes and crooked dimples. Plain stupid, that's what she'd been. Gabby stomped her foot a bit harder, the loose rocks from the edge of the road bumpy under her flats. She'd let her head be turned, just as she had with Blake, but she wouldn't any longer.

Gabby plodded up the stairs to her apartment. She dug out her key from her purse and unlocked the door. She jerked off the sundress and pulled on jeans and a T-shirt.

God, why can't I come out ahead, just once?

Flicking the tears away, Gabby shoved off the pity-party mentality. Feeling sorry for herself wasn't going to help anyone, least of all her.

She mulled things over. So, there had been threats. And the sheriff found out about them. And what was the connection to her?

Gabby jumped into her rental and headed into work. Within minutes, she headed west on Shannon Street. As she passed Sam's Steakhouse, she couldn't resist checking the parking lot for Clark's car. Sure enough, parked in the same space as before, the red Mercedes sparkled under the restaurant's security lights.

Gabby gunned the accelerator. The faster she got to the station, the quicker she could begin her search and the sooner she could get some answers. She parked the rental in her regular spot, took a moment to note Eric's car wasn't there and locked the vehicle before yanking open the door to KLUV.

Immediately, the soft tunes coming out of the in-house speakers soothed her raw nerves. She truly loved the sweet love ballads, the harmony and slower rhythm.

On her way down the hall, she nodded at David Gray in the studio booth. Gabby grabbed her call-in forms, stowed her purse in her locker, then carried her laptop and slipped into the studio where David gave his promo ending.

He slipped off the headset and queued up the station identification announcement that would run on air for nine minutes with the added commercial loops. "How goes it, Gabby?"

"Good, good. How're things with you?"

David stood and stretched. "Just wondering if we're all gonna be standing in the unemployment line before all this mess is over and done." He grabbed his coffee mug and moved from behind the desk.

Gabby shook her head. Poor David, he had a wife and five—count 'em, five—kids who depended on him. Depended on his job at the station for income. For the first time, she realized how fortunate they were that Clark had taken over. If Robert had still been the owner at the time of the attack against him and Howard, who knows how things would have gone. Clark had stepped in just enough to assure Mystique that KLUV was still up and running, and had then stepped back to let them do their jobs. She was grateful for that…if it lasted. But now she was less sure than ever what Clark had planned.

"Eric was all worked up when he left earlier." David rested his hand on the doorknob to the studio. "I wonder if Mr. McKay will scrap us all and bring in new personalities." He threw her a lopsided smile. "We may soon be out of our jobs."

The lump in Gabby's throat seemed to expand. "I don't think so." But she couldn't be sure. She didn't really know Clark at all.

David's smile didn't quite reach his eyes. "Yeah, well, we'll see. 'Night, Gabby." The door shut behind him with a final click.

She set up her laptop and then slipped the headset over her ears just as the commercial loop ended. After giving her opening spiel, she flipped on the first song before accessing the Internet. With a few clicks, Gabby had access to pages upon pages of information on none other than Clark McKay.

Amid the dedication calls and on-air segments, she continued her research. She clicked on yet another link, and her chest contracted. This was it—pay dirt. Hunching over the keyboard, Gabby read as fast as she could about the controversial story. Controversial was an understatement. He'd written an exposé about corruption in Pennsylvania's state government. As a result of the story, several politicians had resigned. Gabby chewed her bottom lip.

She aired two more love dedications before turning back to the laptop. Clicking on another link, Gabby froze as a picture loaded on the page. It was Clark, looking very suave and debonair in a designer tuxedo…and a very beautiful woman, with her hand tucked into the crook of Clark's arm. Gabby narrowed her eyes as she zoomed in on the fine print under the picture.

Clark McKay and attorney Marissa Williams.

So he'd had to hire an attorney. Did he have to hire such a beautiful one? A hot, throbbing ache burned against Gabby's side. She forced herself to scroll down the Web page. Nothing about any threats. Yet another photo loaded, and her lungs trapped her breath, holding it hostage. He looked so sad in the picture announcing the sale of his newspaper.

She went through the motions of announcing more dedications and then set the player to go through two songs and a commercial loop, but her mind remained focused on Clark McKay. And the threats?

What kind of threats were they anyway? Nothing reported about any threats. Not in any of the gazillion articles she scanned. Her frustration mounted as she searched.

The song ended, and Gabby looped into the station identification piece. After that, she flipped on the song waiting. A soft love ballad came over the airwaves and into the station. The phone line blinked. Gabby grabbed her pen and lifted the receiver. "KLUV, this is Gabby. Tell me what's on your heart."

"There's this woman I'd really like to get to know better, but I think I've made her mad at me." The man's voice seemed familiar, but she couldn't place it for certain. Surely it wouldn't be Bubba Moncrief calling about Callie leaving him again.

"Did you do something to offend her?" Gabby kept her tone even.

"Not intentionally. You see, I kept some information from her, thinking I was protecting her."

Not Bubba. Yet the voice was so memorable to her. But who? "Let me guess, she found out and disagreed?"

"That's right. I never meant to hurt her, but I don't know how to win back her trust."

Recognition smacked her in the head. No, he couldn't be calling her here, tonight, at work. Not now.

"Gabby?"

Oh, yeah, it was him. The insufferable Yankee. The man who seemed to live to thwart her chances at happiness.

"Mr. McKay, I'm at work. I'd appreciate you not calling me."

"Wait! Gabby, I'm sorry. I didn't mean to keep things from you."

"Did you call in for a dedication, sir?"

"What?"

"This is the dedication line."

Silence filled the connection. Maybe he'd hung up on her. She hoped so. Then a loud sigh sounded. He was still there, waiting to pounce again. "Thank you for calling, sir."

"Gabby—" Too late, she clicked off the connection.

The music faded, and Gabby clenched her teeth. Call and bother her at work, would he? Keep important information to himself, would he? Well, she would have the last word. At least for tonight.

She switched on her mic. "Mystique, I have a *very special* dedication going out tonight for a new resident to Mystique. Mr. Clark McKay, if you're still listening, this one's for you."

The smile felt good. She pushed the button to start the music, and the recognizable beat of Nancy Sinatra's "These Boots Are Made for Walkin'" oozed from the speakers.

If there was one thing she was certain about, it was that she could outwit any Yankee with her eyes closed.

The peppy song filled his living room. Clark glared at the stereo for a moment, then burst out laughing. Hearty and out loud. "These Boots Are Made for Walkin'"…very good. Game, set and match to Gabby. She'd bested him fair and square.

On this round.

She might have won the battle—and won it well, he had to concede—but the war had just begun. And Clark intended to be victorious.

Despite Gabby Rogillio.

"So, tell me what happened. I've never heard you use your position for personal agendas." Immy's stern voice echoed over the phone.

"Thanks." Gabby sniffed, then proceeded to fill her friend in on what she'd learned.

"I can't believe he didn't tell me. I had to find it out from Sheriff McGruder." Her heart cracked at the thought of Clark's betrayal, and her stupidity in allowing herself to be deceived.

"Great day in the morning, Gab. Maybe he just hadn't found a chance to tell you."

"And yet he had time to hear about my brother's obsession with cars?" Gabby shook her head. "I think not. He should have told me. Especially if the threats involved me this time."

"Look, Gab, I don't know what's going on. I don't have the answers. But I do know people, and I know you." Immy sighed over the phone. "And I love you, Gabby Rogillio, but you and I both know you're quick to anger and judge."

Gabby opened her mouth to protest, but stopped. Was that the truth?

A light lit up on the phone.

"Immy, I've got calls coming in. I'll talk to you tomorrow."

She pressed the flashing button on the phone. "KLUV, this is Gabby. Do you have a dedication?"

"Stop looking into Howard's murder." The male voice crept over the line.

Her heart raced. "Who is this?"

"Stop, or else." An abrupt click snapped against her ear.

Another warning? Even McGruder couldn't deny the connection this time. She lifted the receiver again, this time punching in the number for the sheriff's office.

Her mind attempted to wrap around everything. Whoever slashed her tires and called her had to be the killer. Was it the same person who cut Clark's brake lines and vandalized his house? But how could that tie into the problems Clark had faced before? A Philadelphia criminal would have no reason to hurt Howard or Robert.

After a moment, Sheriff McGruder came on the line. Gabby

told him about the call, sure he'd see reason. But he didn't. He told her he'd file a report, but there wasn't much he could do about an obscene phone call. His voice told her that he didn't really believe her.

The warning alarm signaled the end of the commercial loop. Gabby slammed down the phone and aired two more dedications. Time to get serious. Someone was threatening *her* now.

And she didn't like it.

THIRTEEN

Gabby had every right to be angry. And Clark needed to do whatever it took to make it up to her. But he was scared, scared that his deceit had cost his chance for a relationship. It surprised him to admit he was ready for a romantic entanglement. But Gabby was special.

God, give me the strength and wisdom to make this up to her.

She moved across the parking lot.

"I want to talk to you for a minute."

Gabby glared at him. The morning sun glistened overhead. "Look, I've had a long shift and I'm ready to get home."

"Please."

Something made her stop. "What is it, Clark?"

He covered the distance between them, his heart racing. "I'm sorry I didn't mention the threats. The ones from Philly or the one I got here."

"What kind of threats were they?"

"Look, why don't we go to Ms. Minnie's and have breakfast? I'll tell you everything."

She cocked her head and studied him.

Lord, please encourage her to give me a chance.

"Please, Gabby. I promise I wasn't trying to keep anything from you."

She hesitated, then her shoulders slumped free of their defensive stance. "Fine. I'll follow you there."

In less than ten minutes, they were seated at the back corner of the diner and their breakfast orders taken.

Now he had to bare his soul. Would she rip his heart apart?

"Okay, tell me."

"I wrote a piece about the corruption in Pennsylvania's government."

"I know."

He hitched a brow. "You know?"

Heat crept up the back of her neck. "Amazing what you can find out on the Internet."

"Then you know what I wrote caused several people to resign."

"Yeah."

Ms. Minnie delivered their breakfasts and quickly left to attend to the other patrons. Gabby offered up grace, then she waited on Clark to continue.

"Everything I wrote was factual. One hundred percent. But the politicians' supporters didn't like me running the story." He took a bite of an omelet.

"I imagine not. But if it was the truth—"

"It was, but I wouldn't reveal my sources. So even my friends badgered me. Called me a liar. A mudslinger. Worse."

The pain on his face caused sympathy to edge her heart. She nibbled on her toast. "And they threatened you?"

He ran a hand over his face. "We never knew who threatened me. The police investigated, per se, but really didn't follow up until after everyone implicated admitted what I'd written was true. Then they tried to work the case, but it was too late."

"What were the threats? Could they be related to what's happening here?"

"I really don't think so, Gabby. The threats were calls and letters to me, telling me if I knew what was good for me, I'd leave town." He took a quick sip of coffee. "They stopped after everyone resigned. And the threat from when my house was trashed…it just said that I had to leave or I wouldn't be the only one to get hurt. I suspected that last part referred to you—and it looks like the sheriff agrees—but I didn't want to worry you since I couldn't be sure."

He looked so remorseful. Her heart really ached for him. "I understand. I'm sorry for jumping to conclusions. Seems I'm doing that a lot lately."

"No harm, no foul." He lifted his coffee mug. "So, how was your shift?"

She told him about the caller and McGruder's lack of concern. Everything about his demeanor changed.

"You should've called me."

She shook her head. "Nothing you could do. McGruder couldn't do anything. But we're missing something, Clark."

He frowned at the window. Gabby followed his stare into the parking lot.

A staggering figure wove along the middle of Shannon Street. In the morning glare, drivers would be unable to see him.

Gabby tossed a couple of bills on the table while Clark slid out of the booth. Together, they ran toward the swaying figure. "Sir, are you okay?" Gabby hollered, just as the wind kicked in her direction.

The overpowering stench of liquor nearly made her gag, but she continued toward the inebriated man.

Gabby leaned forward, peering into his face. "Sam? Sam Wood?"

The man's head jerked.

"Oh, Mr. Sam. What have you done?" She crossed to the man's other side. "It's me, Gabby Rogillio." Her arm wove around his waist, and she tucked his arm over her shoulder.

Clark mimicked her movements until they led the drunken man toward her rental.

"I'm sorry, Ms. Gabby. I just had a few beers to ease my pain," Sam mumbled, filling the air with his foul stench.

"Whew, Mr. Sam, you smell like a brewery. Beer this early in the morning?"

Clark shifted to take the older man's weight while Gabby struggled to open the rental's back door.

Gabby helped secure Mr. Sam in the backseat before slipping behind the driver's wheel. She whispered to Clark, "I've never seen Mr. Sam drink at all."

Clark shrugged. "I wonder what he's doing in the middle of the road, three sheets to the wind, this early in the morning."

"Probably been out all night." Gabby glanced into her rearview mirror. "Mr. Sam. Mr. Sam, can you tell me what's wrong?"

"So senseless. Broke my heart." The man began to sob, his bald spot prominent in the reflection of the dashboard lights. "We were so in *looovve.*"

Clark looked to Gabby. "What's he talking about?"

"Haven't a clue." She turned the rental into his driveway. "Here we are."

After the vehicle rolled to a stop, Gabby and Clark fought to get Sam from the backseat and up the stairs. His steps faltered several times.

"Mr. Sam, where's your house key?"

"Not locked," he muffled as he swayed.

Gabby braced against the doorjamb for support and turned the knob. Sure enough, it opened. Yet another nice thing about living in a small town—most people didn't feel the need to lock their doors, they trusted their neighbors. She helped Clark drag Mr. Sam into the house.

"It's sad. That good-for-nothing Robert Ellison. All his fault," Sam said as they lowered him to the couch.

Gabby's heart skipped a beat. "What's that about Robert Ellison?" Maybe she could finally get to the root of Sam's grudge against Robert.

Sam looked at her, his wrinkled face marred with sadness. The corners of his dark eyes drooped to meet the crow's feet. "He stole Amber from me. And now he's given her this latest misery. The dirty rat."

"What are you saying, Mr. Sam?" She lowered herself to the chair across from the couch. "You and Amber were once an item?" She'd never heard of it.

He nodded. "All through high school. She was my girl, Ms. Gabby. We was so in love." Liquor had thickened his tongue.

She laid a hand on his. "I didn't know. What happened?"

"We planned to get married soon as we graduated. We'd already been busy playing house, if you catch my drift." Sam waggled his gray, bushy eyebrows. "But then, at the end of our senior year, right after graduation, Amber up and disappeared." Fat tears fell from his eyes.

Gabby cleared her throat. "Where'd she go?"

Sam pawed at the tears on his cheeks. "To visit relatives over in Louisiana. Someplace down in Calcasieu Parish—Cajun country. She was gone a whole year."

"But she came back…" Gabby patted his hand.

"When she did, she was married to that uppity Robert Ellison."

Clark squatted in front of Sam. "Did she give you any reason? Any kind of explanation?"

Swaying, Sam leaned back against the couch. "Never said a

single thing. Wouldn't even talk to me." His voice lowered, his words trailed off. "That…sorry son of a…"

Sam didn't finish his statement. Didn't even move.

"Mr. Sam?" Gabby shook the man's hand.

A loud snore erupted from Sam, followed by a snort.

Clark stood. "He's passed out. He won't tell us anything else."

"I guess not." She headed to the door. "Come on, let's go."

"Did you know? About him and Amber and Robert, I mean?" Clark paused by the front door.

"I've lived in Mystique all my life and never heard that story." Gabby shrugged as she crossed the front porch.

She stared at the passed-out Sam Wood. Without meaning to, the man had just provided himself with a motive for setting up Robert. But did he have anything against Howard? She pulled the door closed and followed Clark down the stairs.

Gabby drove Clark back to the diner. "I can't process anything more until I get some sleep."

He smiled. "Go home and get some rest. I'll talk to you on your shift."

She returned the grin. "Better watch out. I don't know how my new boss feels about employee fraternization."

Leaning over the car's console, Clark whispered, "I think I can handle him."

And then he wrapped his hand in her hair and drew her close. Closer. Dipped his head and pressed his lips against hers.

Soft at first. Then harder. More demanding.

Her head spun. She jerked back, breathless.

He chuckled. "Sweet dreams, Gabby." Clark opened the door and was gone.

Leaving Gabby confused and her adrenaline racing.

* * *

Clark pulled into Aunt Beulah's driveway as night settled securely over Mystique. With all the chaos lately, he hadn't been visiting as much as he should. Something about his great-aunt always soothed him, and he needed some calm right now.

She opened the screen door before he even cleared the stairs. "What's buggin' you, boy?" She tightened the belt of her robe.

Was his distress so plain to see? He planted a kiss on his aunt's cheek and followed her into the house. "I didn't check the time, Aunt Beulah. Were you in bed?"

She waved him into the living room. "Of course not. I'm old, but not bedridden. I always watch the late news." Aunt Beulah plopped into her worn recliner. "What's givin' you fits?"

"My life." Clark lowered himself to the couch.

She chuckled. "What else is new, boy? Would you care to be more specific?"

"So much is happening so fast."

"What's that?"

"All the hoopla with the station that I now own. My brake lines being cut. My house being trashed."

She removed her glasses and wiped them on the hem of her tired robe, then shoved them back over the bridge of her nose. "Sounds like someone don't like you much, son."

"I guess not. But now an employee is receiving threats, too. So it's not just me."

"Did you tell Sheriff McGruder? It's his job to protect the citizens of this town, not your responsibility. Employees are just that—employees." She peered at him over the rim of her glasses.

He fought the urge to fidget. His aunt always had been able to cut through all the layers to hit the core of a problem. "Well, she's…well…"

"Gabby." Aunt Beulah nodded.

"Yes, but how'd—"

"I'm old, not blind, boy." She chuckled. "Gabby's got a right mind of her own, that girl surely does."

Wasn't that the truth? "But someone's threatening her now, too."

"Tragedies can bring out the worst in people. Just like it has for poor Sam Wood. From what I heard today, his horns are showing since Robert's arrest."

"Gabby and I just saw him, dead drunk, crying about how Robert stole Amber from him."

"Can't say as I blame him for holding a grudge, considering how things went back then."

Clark's heart shifted into a higher gear. "What do you mean?"

Aunt Beulah leaned her head against the recliner. "Reckon I should just tell you what we all heard back then, what we all believed to be true."

Remaining silent, Clark willed his heart to stop thudding too loudly in his head so he could hear his aunt's words.

"Where to start?" She waved a hand. "No matter. The truth is that Sam Wood was devastated when Amber left town. Never seen a man so down and out." Aunt Beulah glanced out the window, as if losing focus. "Everyone expected them to marry someday, but instead she ended things before leaving town. Rumor had it that Amber had found out she was pregnant by Sam and left to have the baby. Sure enough, she came back almost twelve months later."

Clark couldn't let his aunt finish. "Did she? Have a baby, I mean?"

Thunder rumbled in the distance. Lightning speared the sky. Aunt Beulah glanced to the heavens, then back at Clark. "No one knows for certain, child, except Amber herself. Oh, nobody ever asked her, and none of us ever breathed a word of our suspicions to poor Sam. Bless his heart, he was torn up enough as it was."

She sighed. "So that's the sad story, child. Now, I don't know for certain the truth, but it sure made sense of her long departure."

She stared at Clark. "You take that information, son, and you be careful with it."

"Thank you, Aunt Beulah. I really appreciate it."

"You do what's right, and nothing more, you hear?"

Brring!

Clark grabbed his cell phone from his hip. "Just a minute." He didn't recognize the number on the caller ID, but it was local. "Hello."

"Mr. McKay?"

"Yes."

"This is Walter with Mystique Security." The company Clark had hired for security at KLUV this afternoon.

"Yes?"

"I noticed a white Lincoln Town Car parked in the lot. Didn't think much about it, until I made my second pass and saw a figure inside. I headed that direction, and it left."

Someone in the parking lot, at night, when Gabby was at the station by herself… "Did the person ever get out?" Clark stood, fishing out his keys.

"Not that I know. Like I said, as soon as they saw me, they took outta here. I got a partial on the license plate."

"Just watch for it and call the police if it returns. I'm on my way now."

"Yes, sir."

Clark reattached the cell to his hip clip. "Sorry I have to run off, Aunt Beulah, but there's something strange going on around KLUV."

"I understand. Go on and take care of your business, boy."

He started his car and backed out of the driveway as the rain began to fall. Who'd been nosing around the station? Was the killer back, looking for another target?

And Gabby was all alone at the station.

FOURTEEN

Crack!

Gabby set the coffee cup in the sink in the break room and rushed to the front door. What on Earth?

The front of Martin Tankersly's Lincoln Town Car had plowed into the side of Clark McKay's sporty little Mercedes-Benz.

She twisted the dead bolt and opened the door just as Mr. Tankersly hopped from his car. His thinning hair plastered to his round head in the rain. "Are you blind?" He strode forward. "You stupid idiot."

Clark climbed from his car. "Sir, you hit me."

Mr. Tankersly glanced at the front end of his car shoved into Clark's. He lifted his eyes, hatred burning. "You pulled out in front of me! You weren't watching where you were going." He jerked a hand toward the automobiles. "Just look at my car—what you did."

"You hit me. You were racing out of the parking lot." Clark reached for his cell phone. "But that's what insurance companies are for. Just let me call mine…"

Gabby took a step out of the station as Mr. Tankersly stormed Clark, slugging him in the jaw and knocking him to the ground.

She gasped as she moved toward the men, but Clark quickly recovered, causing her to stop. What was she thinking—about to get between them and break up the brawl? Had she lost her ever-loving mind?

Jumping up, Clark stared at Mr. Tankersly amid the rain. "Are you insane? What're you doing?"

"You wrecked my car." Mr. Tankersly took another step toward him.

A sedan, bearing the logo of a local security company, screeched to a halt adjacent to the wreck. A man in uniform jumped out. "Mr. McKay, are you all right? I called the sheriff just as you said."

"I'm fine." Clark sidestepped, shifting as Mr. Tankersly's thundering fist sailed through the air. He glared at the man. "Are you drunk?"

Mr. Tankersly rushed for Clark, but slipped on the slick concrete. His legs flew out from under him, and he crashed to the ground.

A lone siren wailed.

"You need to calm down, man." Clark stepped out of arm's length of Tankersly, who drew to his feet. "It was an accident."

Mr. Tankersly lunged for Clark.

The security man dove for Mr. Tankersly.

Gabby pressed her fingers to her mouth. Oh, good gravy. This was going to turn into a knock-down, drag-out fight. Where was McGruder when you actually needed him?

"You yellerbelly Yankee! I knew it—spineless and stupid." Spittle flew from the corners of Mr. Tankersly's sagging mouth. He jerked forward, hands balled into fists.

Clark moved around the guard and swung with his right hand. Mr. Tankersly dropped to the ground with a loud thud, followed by a grunt. Clark shook his hand.

Mr. Tankersly spit, red mixing with the puddles of rain forming in the indentations of the parking lot. He turned to his hands and knees, pushing to his feet.

"Stop!"

All three men turned to stare at her. Gabby slunk back against the building, shocked she'd screamed aloud.

The siren wailed louder as the sheriff's cruiser whipped alongside the wrecked cars. High time he made an appearance.

Sheriff McGruder, with a large hat perched on his head, strode over to the men. "What's going on here, boys?"

"This Yankee totaled my car. Just look at it, Sheriff," Mr. Tankersly growled and swayed.

"Why's your lip bleeding, Martin?" Sheriff McGruder narrowed his eyes. "Were you injured in the accident? Want me to call the paramedics?"

"Nah." Mr. Tankersly spit again, then glared at Clark. "He hit me."

"He hit me first. I was just defending myself." Clark held up his hands.

"That's true, Sheriff." Gabby joined the men. Rain pelted her head, driving against the migraine forming. "Mr. Tankersly hit Mr. McKay's car with his, then stormed out throwing punches."

The shock of seeing a fistfight up close and personal had her emotions all knotted.

"That's the truth, Sheriff. And this gentleman's car here is the one I called and reported," the other man said.

"Who are you?" asked McGruder.

"Walter. Walter Robinson, Mystique Security."

"You been drinking, Martin?" the sheriff asked.

"I ain't been drinking." Mr. Tankersly's eyes narrowed as he glared at Gabby. "And this wasn't my fault."

"Why, Mr. Tankersly, that's an out-and-out lie." Gabby fisted her hands onto her hips.

"Shut up." He spat again, then turned his focus on Clark.

"This is all your fault. Stupid Yankee, I'll teach you to stay north of the Mason-Dixon Line…"

Faster than Gabby would have thought possible, Mr. Tankersly pushed toward Clark, fists flying.

A whack sounded as his fist collided with Clark's cheekbone. Instantly, Clark threw his own punch, landing squarely on Martin Tankersly's nose. Blood spurted.

"That'll be about enough." Sheriff McGruder yanked Mr. Tankersly by his shoulder, spinning him around to lay him facedown against the trunk of the Town Car. "Martin Tankersly, you have the right to remain silent—anything you say can and will be used against you in a court of law…"

The sheriff's monotone as he recited the Miranda rights droned on in Gabby's ears. She didn't pay attention, she moved to touch Clark's shoulder. "Oh, dear. Let me get you some ice." Men. "I'll be right back."

She hurried to the break room where she yanked a Baggie and filled it with ice. She turned and rushed to the parking lot, handing the homemade ice pack to Clark, who pressed it against his cheek and cringed.

"You want to press assault charges, Mr. McKay?" The sheriff had finished telling Mr. Tankersly his rights, and had handcuffed the man.

Clark nodded. "I believe I will."

"You'll need to come down to the station and fill out a report."

"Okay."

The sheriff waved toward the vehicles. "I don't think yours can be moved until I get Martin's hauled away."

"I'll call a tow truck." Clark faced Gabby again. "Walter called me and reported Mr. Tankersly driving around the station's lot. I told him to call the sheriff." The bruise already forming on his cheek marred his disarming smile. "With a murderer still on the loose, I hired security." He glared at Mr. Tankersly. "Good thing I did, too."

"Gabby?" Sheriff McGruder interrupted.

She spun and faced him. "Yes?" Realizing how sharp her retort came out, she tossed him a feeble smile.

"Have you noticed Martin driving around the station?"

"No. But I'm in the studio most all the time. I was getting a refill on coffee when I heard the cars collide."

The sheriff turned to Mr. Tankersly. "Why were you here, Martin?"

"Eric called and told me to meet him here at eleven."

"That's a lie." Gabby stared at Sheriff McGruder. "Eric would never have asked Mr. Tankersly to meet him here. Eric doesn't like him."

"I've heard enough. We'll sort this out at the station. I'll talk to Eric." Sheriff McGruder pulled Mr. Tankersly toward the rear of the police car. "Come on, Martin. Let's not make this any harder."

"Listening to a Yankee—what kind of sheriff are you, any-way?" He twisted to stare over at Clark. "And you...you're as no good as that stupid adopted son of my dead wife. Good riddance to you all."

Sheriff McGruder shoved Mr. Tankersly in the backseat of the cruiser, then slammed the door shut. "Mr. McKay, I'll need you to come to the station with us now to fill out the complaint." He moved to the door. "We can call a tow truck from the station."

"Yes, sir." Clark hesitated as he stared at Gabby. "I'll call you later."

"Walter and Gabby, you'll need to come make statements as witnesses. It can wait until tomorrow." Sheriff McGruder slipped behind the wheel of the cruiser.

The security guard nodded, then headed to his car.

"Okay." Gabby wove her fingers in front of her.

"You can pick up your vehicle then, too. We finished processing it today."

But she wasn't listening anymore. Her mind was still caught on what Martin Tankersly had yelled out.

Adopted son of Mr. Tankersly's dead wife? Who was that?

McGruder interrupted her thoughts. "You don't worry about the investigation, Gabby. That's what we do. This has nothing to do with that prank call." He tugged the door to almost closed. "Don't forget to come by my office and sign your statement."

Gabby nodded, then slipped inside the station, clicking the dead bolt into place. *Could* Mr. Tankersly have been the one who called her? The voice on the phone had sounded almost familiar…but the call had been so short, it was hard to tell. And she hadn't been able to stop and think about it for long since she'd been in the middle of her pro—her program! She raced back toward the studio. The silence filling the station sent her heart thumping.

The controls sat as silent as the dead air going out over the frequency waves. The phone lights, however, blinked up as rapidly as a Christmas tree.

Gabby slammed the headset over her ears and queued up her microphone. "Sorry, Mystique. The station is experiencing technical difficulties." She pressed the button to play the next song, her heart sinking to her toes. One of her worst fears had just come to life…she'd allowed dead air time on KLUV. Advertisers would pull their sponsorships.

Not to mention the effect this would have on her show being syndicated.

And Clark could fire her.

In the front seat of the sheriff's cruiser, Clark opened his cell phone. Anything to drown out Mr. Tankersly's tirade from the backseat. Clark refused to argue with the man. Instead, he accessed the Internet, then went to his music selection menu. He selected KLUV and waited for it to load. Maybe it was silly to listen to the radio via his cell phone, but it made him feel somewhat closer to Gabby. Right now, he wanted to hear her voice, to make sure she was okay.

What was that comment about a prank phone call? He glanced at the sheriff, weighing his options. If he asked, McGruder probably wouldn't tell him. Gabby was right—the sheriff didn't take it seriously.

His phone indicated the connection had been made, but only silence sat in the speakers. Then Gabby's throaty voice apologized for the station's technical difficulties before music hit the waves.

She wasn't okay. No deejay would allow dead airtime if they could avoid it. Yet she had. The incident with Martin Tankersly had upset her more than he'd thought. Or the call had her rattled. Either way, Clark needed to get to her—see for himself that she was okay.

Within twenty minutes, he'd been delivered to the interview room to wait while the sheriff processed Mr. Tankersly.

The interview room in the sheriff's office was hot. And smelly. Clark leaned back against the metal chair and stared at the mirror. The one he knew was a two-way. While he waited for McGruder to come back with official complaint paperwork, he called his insurance company and reported the accident, had a tow truck lined up to get his car to Lou's, and requested a rental be delivered to the sheriff's office. All completed, and still he waited.

The sheriff entered at his normal slow pace and set a stack of papers on the table. "I'll need you to fill these out."

Clark reached for the pen. "So, what does Mr. Tankersly have to say? Why was he at the station?"

"Not that it's any of your business, but he claims Eric Masters asked him to meet him there."

Tightening his grip on the pen, Clark struggled to keep his tone even. "Actually, since I own KLUV, it *is* my business why the man was on my property."

Sheriff McGruder straightened his shoulders. "So it is, Mr. McKay. Either way, that's his story. I'll call Eric in the morning to get his side."

"Don't you find this all odd, Sheriff? That Mr. Tankersly was loitering around my station late at night for no good reason? Can't you just consider that there's something more going on than an open-and-shut case against Mr. Ellison?"

"Why don't you leave the investigating to me, Mr. McKay?"

"And if Tankersly's lying?"

"Then I'll get to the bottom of what he was doing there."

"What about Gabby's slashed tires?"

"What about them?"

"Did you find any fingerprints or anything on the vehicle?"

"That really *is* none of your business." The sheriff tapped the table. "Just bring those to the officer at the desk when you're done. Lou sent over a rental right away. It's parked in the lot and the officer up front has the keys."

Which meant the conversation was over. No sense asking more.

Sheriff McGruder ambled from the room, leaving the door open. Clark completed the forms, then took them to the front desk. He picked up the rental car keys from the officer, then headed out the front door.

A light drizzle coated his head and shoulders. He slipped into the car with the rental plates, cranked the engine, and then adjusted the radio to KLUV's frequency.

"…so call me, Mystique, and share your loves and longings. I'm Gabby Rogillio, here to play your dedications."

Her voice was a life preserver in a stormy sea. Clark slipped the car in Reverse, checked his rearview mirror, then backed out of the parking space. While Gabby's shift would be ending in a couple of hours, he steered toward KLUV. He could always use the excuse of giving her the information he'd learned from Aunt Beulah.

But he knew that was merely an excuse. Somewhere in the middle of it all, Gabby Rogillio had snuck under his skin.

And stuck there.

He waved at Walter when he pulled into the lot, then eased his car slowly around the building. Clark secured the rental, then headed to the entrance. Gabby would be the only one inside, and he didn't want to alarm her.

The piped-in music of KLUV filled the vacant reception area. He'd have to see about hiring a full-time receptionist. Clark had high aspirations for the station, ones that involved a lot of calls, and not just to the dedication lines.

He turned, making his way silently down the hall. The red light over the studio door blazed. He peeked through the window to find Gabby hunched over a laptop, her brows creased. She wore a headset around her neck like an accessory. What could she be concentrating so hard on? With his finger, he tapped on the window.

She jumped, then waved him in. "How's your jaw?"

He closed the studio door behind him and rubbed his chin. "A little sore, but I've had worse." Heart thumping, he dropped to the chair in front of the control center. "How're you?"

"I'm not the one who got into a slugfest in the parking lot."

"Touché. I found out something today." And he proceeded to tell her what his Aunt Beulah had shared with him about Sam Wood and Amber Ellison.

Confusion glimmered in her eyes as she took care of making more dedications before turning back to him. "I don't know what to make of it all."

"We can't disregard your slashed tires and call, either."

She queued another song, then stared back at him.

"I asked the sheriff if he'd found any fingerprints or trace evidence on your vehicle."

"And?"

Clark shrugged. "He wouldn't tell me. Said it was none of my business."

"Sounds about right for McGruder. You'd have thought he would've called me earlier today to let me know I could pick up my truck instead of just adding it as an afterthought to ordering me to the station tomorrow."

"True." He waited while she did her deejay thing again, then smiled. "So I think we have a starting place for our investigation. Sam Wood's and Amber Ellison's past."

"Clark, why did you hire a security guard?"

Because I'm insanely attracted to you? Probably wouldn't be the brightest idea to blurt that out just yet. "Because I want to get the truth before someone else gets hurt."

He couldn't take it if anything happened to any of the employees. But especially Gabby.

FIFTEEN

Gabby flipped the switch to loop a commercial set. She glanced at the clock—barely an hour left on her shift. "Okay. Let's look at it this way—Sam Wood had every reason to hate Robert." Just stating that felt wrong. "Is there a link between Sam and Howard?"

Clark leaned back in the chair, his expression less tense. "You're the local. Have you ever heard of anything?"

"No, but I had no clue about Sam and Amber, either."

"I could ask my aunt." He glanced at the clock. "But she won't be up for a couple more hours."

She snapped her fingers. "Sheldon."

"What's Sheldon got to do with this?"

She giggled. "She's Mystique's librarian. I bet she could dig around and see if there's any connection between them."

"But it's not even six in the morning."

"Sheldon gets up at four-thirty to do her yoga routine." She reached for the phone and pressed numbers, keeping an eye on the on-air loop. Two minutes and fourteen seconds left.

"What's up, Gab?" Sheldon always checked her caller ID before answering.

"I need a favor." Two minutes and two seconds left.

Sheldon's throaty laugh filled the connection. "Well, I didn't think you'd call me this early for my tea biscuit recipe."

Gabby laughed, her spirits lifted just by hearing her friend's voice. "Good point."

"Whatcha need?"

"I need you to search everything you can and see if you can find a connection between Sam Wood and Howard Alspeed."

"What kind of connection?" Sheldon's voice grew tense.

"Any." One minute and eighteen seconds left.

"I'll see what I can find. Gab, what's going on?"

One minute left. "Long story. I'll fill you in later."

"You got it."

"Thanks, Shel. Really appreciate it." Thirty-two seconds left.

"Call you when I find something."

Gabby hung up, settled the headphones over her ears and pressed her mic button. "This is Gabby Rogillio, thanking you for tuning in tonight and sharing your love stories with me. Join me again tonight at ten, when I'll send out more of your love dedications. Until then, live and love well, Mystique." She clicked off the on-air button, queued up KLUV's station identification announcement and slipped off the headset.

"And that's it?" Clark shoved to his feet.

"That's it." She stood and stretched, her back aching. "Kevin should be here by now. If he's on time." She reached for her case.

"Is he late often?" Clark stood beside her.

"Enough." She froze as she set the timer to how much time was left on the circle of announcements. "I keep forgetting you're the boss now. I don't want to get him into trouble."

"Don't worry about it." But his brow tightened.

"Clark, I can't worry about being around you if I'm going to have to watch everything I say. In case you haven't noticed, I have a tendency to spout off when the emotion hits me." Heat tickled her face as he smiled.

Great. She had to be as transparent as the window.

Luckily, Kevin chose that moment to barge into the studio. "Hey, Gabby. Hiya, Mr. McKay." He flopped into the chair, jerked the headphones over his ears and queued up his mic. "Good morning, Mystique. This is Kevin Duffy, here to take you through rush hour. I'll be back with you in a jiffy to give you a weather and traffic update. Until then, here's something to get you rolling." He pressed a lever and the opening bars of "I Can't Drive 55" filled the air.

Gabby shook her head and led Clark from the studio. Kevin might be unorthodox, but morning listeners seemed to love him. Didn't flinch from his taking over Howard's time slot.

Speaking of Howard…his funeral had yet to be set due to the fact that his extended family had to be located. Otherwise, friends would have to arrange his funeral.

The knot in Gabby's gut tightened. Maybe Sheldon would find a connection.

Soon.

The rain came down harder as Gabby ran to her SUV parked in the back of the sheriff's office. Her shirt stuck to her back, but she preferred the rain to the intensity of filing her report with McGruder. His lack of finding any evidence on her vehicle reeked of inadequacy. After starting the engine, she laid her forehead against the steering wheel and closed her eyes. What a morning.

Lord, I'm drowning down here. Show me what to do.

Her cell phone beeped.

"Hello."

"Hey, Gab. Whatcha doing?" Imogene's sweet voice made Gabby smile.

She slipped the vehicle in gear and pulled onto the road. "Just leaving the sheriff's office from getting my truck back. What're you doing?"

"Calling to see if you wanted to meet for lunch."

Ah, Immy's in-tune radar was right on target. "I'd love that."

"Meet me at Ms. Minnie's?"

"On my way."

The drive only took ten minutes. Little gusts of wind shoved water everywhere, soaking Gabby as she rushed into the diner.

"Lands a-mighty, child, you look like a drowned rat." Ms. Minnie passed her monogrammed handkerchief to Gabby.

"Thanks." Gabby dabbed at her face while heading to the booth in the corner. "Can I get some coffee, Ms. Minnie?"

"Go ahead on back, honey. I'll be right there."

Gabby hugged Imogene before sitting down. "I'm so glad you called me for lunch."

"What's wrong?"

"You just always seem to know when I need a little of your TLC."

"What's happened now?" What Immy's eyes lacked in luster, they more than made up for with expressing emotion.

"What hasn't happened? Let's see, Mr. Tankersly and Clark got into a wreck, then a fistfight last night at the station."

"Great day in the morning! What happened?"

Gabby filled her friend in on the events, then smiled as Ms. Minnie poured her a cup of steaming, aromatic coffee. She handed the sweet lady her handkerchief back.

"Special today is chicken-fried steak." Ms. Minnie straightened.

Gabby's mouth watered. "Oh, that sounds great. I'll take it."

"Me, too," Immy piped up.

"Be right out."

"So," Immy dumped cream into her coffee and then straightened the creamer next to the sugar tray. "What else?"

Gabby blew into her cup, the heat bouncing back against her face a welcome relief to the cool rain seeping into her bones. "Oh. And get this." She took a quick sip, then set the cup on the table before filling her friend in on what she and Clark had discovered.

"It's nice you two are working together."

"Nice? I don't know about that. I mean, he explained about what happened to him in Philadelphia. Of course, he doesn't want the same thing to happen to Robert."

"So what?" Immy lined the salt and pepper shakers in perfect alignment with the sugar tray. "I still say you're part of the reason he cares so much."

"No. I'm not." Gabby swallowed back the groan.

"Come on, Gab. What do you think I am, blind? I can see the interest and attraction flying between you two like bees to honey." She lowered her voice as she traced the rim of her mug. "Why don't you just admit you're being too hard on Mr. McKay because you're scared?"

"Scared?" Gabby's heart fluttered as her pulse spiked. "What, pray tell, would I be scared of?"

Immy shook her head, her eyes soft and caring. "Scared of letting yourself trust another man. Especially a man involved in your industry."

Gabby swallowed against the now softball-size lump in her chest. Immy was the only one of the girls who knew the whole sorry story of why she'd changed her major from broadcast journalism to radio communications—the only one who knew about how she'd let herself fall in love with a man, only to discover he'd been using her for a story and nothing more.

"Sweetie, it's okay to be wary." Immy laid a comforting hand over hers. "But Clark McKay is not Blake Riggsdale. He's not out to hurt you."

"How can you be sure? We don't know him. He's a Yankee, for pity's sakes."

Immy squeezed her hand. "That doesn't make him a playboy."

Gabby shrugged as Ms. Minnie approached with two plates. "I don't know, but I'll think about it."

"No, pray about it."

Just then, Tonna breezed into the diner and slid into the booth beside Imogene. "Thought I'd find y'all here." She nudged Immy. "I called the clinic, and they said you'd gone to lunch."

"What's up?" Gabby asked.

Tonna's response had to wait as Ms. Minnie approached. Tonna gave her order for the special, and Ms. Minnie shuffled back to the kitchen.

"Ms. LouAnn came in this morning for a rinse." Tonna shook her head. "I swear, that woman just likes to come into town to catch up. Her hair was fine. But she does know what's going on in Mystique, that's for sure."

"Ton-na." Immy waved her fork toward their friend.

"Okay, okay. Anyway, I thought maybe I could get some more information about Mr. Sam from Ms. LouAnn."

Gabby's hope deflated. She already knew about Sam and Amber.

"According to Ms. LouAnn, she and Mr. Tankersly were once an item." Tonna's eyes widened. "Can you imagine?"

Ms. LouAnn and Mr. Tankersly? Would the secret loves of the town's elders never cease to amaze? Gabby shook her head as Ms. Minnie set a steaming plate in front of Tonna, refilled the coffee cups, then headed back to her station behind the counter.

Tonna kept on with her story. "Seems Ms. LouAnn and Mr. Tankersly still talk quite a bit, despite the fact that she says there's nothing more than a platonic friendship between them." She waggled her eyebrows. "Like I'm supposed to believe that?"

"Tonna," Immy admonished.

"Anyhoo, she says Mr. Tankersly tried to hire Howard out from under Robert, but Howard refused." Tonna shoved a bite into her mouth.

"No big surprise there. Howard wouldn't leave because he owned stock in KLUV."

"No, Ms. LouAnn said this was after Howard had sold his stock to Robert. She said Mr. Tankersly was furious. Her exact words were, and I quote, 'Martin was beyond livid. I've never seen him that angry before.' End quote."

Gabby's stomach clenched, and it had nothing to do with Ms. Minnie's cooking.

Brring!

Gabby grabbed her cell, checked the caller ID and answered. "Hey, Shel. What's up?"

"Found a connection between Sam and Howard."

Gabby's heart raced. "What?"

"In the paper from twenty years ago, I'm looking at a picture of Sam and Howard. They were partners in a fishing tournament, and they look rather chummy."

What could that mean? "Shel, is there any information listed in the article about them?"

"Nothing that I can find. I'll keep looking, but you said you were interested in any connection. This picture makes it look like they're the best of friends."

Yet Gabby had never seen them together nor heard Howard even mention Mr. Sam. Had they had a falling-out? "Thanks, Shel. I appreciate it."

But what did it all mean?

Maybe things would turn around this evening. She finished her supper, then headed to work. She hadn't gotten any sleep, and here she was, back at work. The station was as quiet as a tomb. She knocked lightly on Eric's closed office door.

"Come in."

She pushed open the door and studied the station manager. In all the time she'd worked with Eric, she'd never seen him close his office door. She'd also never seen him look quite so undone. "Are you okay? You look a little peaked." Gabby crossed the room and peered at him. "Are you coming down with something?"

He waved off her concern. "I'm fine. Just a little confused over Martin's arrest last night."

"Yeah, it was grim." She sank into the cracked leather chair. "He said you called and asked him to meet you here."

"I'm still wondering what's up with that. As if I'd call him, of all people."

"Who knows? I told McGruder it had to be a lie because you hate him."

"Ain't that the truth." Eric chuckled, but it came out lifeless. "The man never stops thinking of ways to torment me."

"Just him being here is suspicious."

"I know." Eric's eyes hardened, as did his facial expression. "I know I said before that Martin wasn't likely to be involved in the attacks, but if you're convinced it wasn't Robert, maybe it was Martin after all. He has an explosive temper. Bad. And it can get violent."

Her heart broke for the little boy he'd been, the one who'd been abused. "I'm sorry, Eric. I never knew."

"Most people didn't." He shrugged. "He hid it well, and I wasn't one to go around whining. I mean, he was only my step-father—he could have kicked me out anytime after Mom died."

"That's horrible. Do you think he could kill someone?"

"I don't want to think so, but…maybe." Eric ran a hand over

his stubbly chin. "Many times he threatened to kill me if I didn't adhere to his rules."

She leaned to lay her hand over his. "I don't know what else to say except I'm so sorry."

He brushed off her touch. "It's all in the past."

"Yeah." She struggled to stand. "I need to go get my call sheets."

"I'll close this up and then head out."

She grinned and staggered down the hall, her mind reeling with information overload.

After storing her purse in her locker, Gabby flipped out the lights to the break room. She clutched her cup of coffee and call sheets, and strode down the hall to Eric's office.

The lights were out, and Eric was nowhere to be found. The glow from his computer terminal lit the office. Gabby smiled. He forgot to turn off his monitor a lot.

As she made her way into his darkened office, she flipped on the light switch and noticed his suits hanging on the tree stand. He must have left in a hurry, he even forgot his dry cleaning.

She moved past the stand and knocked off one of the covered hangers. Gabby jerked it up and hung it again, smoothing down the transparent plastic. Fingering the creases out, she noticed the dry cleaning slip stapled to the top.

TEAR PATCHED AS BEST AS POSSIBLE. $10.00 REPAIR FEE.

Eric better find himself a woman and get hitched soon—the minor stitching fees were going to eat him alive. Gabby smiled and moved to the desk.

She pressed the button to turn off the monitor. A slip of paper on the floor caught in her peripheral vision. Bending, she retrieved it. Her gaze automatically registered what she held—a deposit slip. As she scanned the amount, Gabby's heart pounded. *Fifty thousand dollars!* She jerked the slip closer and studied the information—the date, the account name and the amount again. Eric's personal account—she knew because she'd made his payroll deposit several times over the years. Where did Eric get fifty thousand dollars to deposit into his account today?

With shaking hands, Gabby shoved the receipt on the edge of the desk, then slipped out of the office.

What was going on?

SIXTEEN

Night fell over Mystique. Clark ducked into Ms. Minnie's diner, then shook off the raindrops spattering his back and shoulders.

Three of Gabby's friends sat at the back booth. He took a moment to realize what a smorgasbord they were—the classic young beauty from the B and B; the librarian, a strawberry-blonde with cold green eyes, and nurse Imogene, the mousy type, but with personality bubbling from her face. So different, but obviously so in tune with one another. As one, their laughter ceased, and they turned to stare at him.

He resisted the urge to squirm. When Clark moved to go to the other side of the diner, Imogene called out to him. "Mr. McKay, won't you join us?"

He glanced at the friends and found the strength to uproot his feet.

Imogene slid over next to the young classical beauty. "Sit."

"Thank you." Clark dropped onto the bench beside the librarian.

"I don't think you've been properly introduced to all the girls, have you?"

"No."

As if she didn't notice his discomfort, Imogene pointed across the table at the woman sitting beside him. "That's Sheldon, town librarian. I believe you met her at the Ellisons'."

He nodded at her.

Imogene tilted her head to the side. "And you've met this lady beside me, Rayne VanDoren, manager of the B and B."

"So, Mr. McKay—" Sheldon pinned him with her scrutiny "—what exactly are your intentions toward Gabby?" Those green eyes of hers could freeze his blood right in his veins.

Heat skidded up his neck and scorched his face. He realized what facing the Spanish Inquisition must have felt like.

"Sheldon! How rude," Imogene admonished.

He couldn't help but chuckle. "It's okay, really."

Good thing, too, because Sheldon didn't look as if she were the least bit fazed by Imogene's reprimand. Her stare remained locked on his face, and even Rayne leaned forward to stare at him over Imogene.

He hauled in a deep breath. "I really like Gabby—a lot—and I want to get to know her better."

"But?" Sheldon jumped right on him, not giving him an inch to collect his thoughts.

He nodded as the waitress approached with a carafe of coffee. Clark waited until she'd filled his cup and walked away before readdressing the ladies. "There's still something she doesn't trust me about. She even refused to look at the house I bought."

A collective hush fell over the table. He glanced at Sheldon, who dropped her gaze to study the French fries drowning in ketchup. He looked at Rayne, whose lips were pressed so tight together, they were white around the edges. Something wasn't right—they knew what was going on.

"What?" He faced Imogene. "Help me out here."

Imogene searched his face.

"I really like her."

Imogene cleared her throat.

"What?" Was he just blind to the obvious? Each woman at the table seemed to sit in shocked silence.

"Well, you see…"

"Immy, you can't tell him Gabby's personal business," Sheldon said with a slap to the tabletop. "She'll kill you."

Clark turned pleading eyes to Imogene. "Please. I really want to understand."

"Look, she had a really bad experience back in college with the management of a local news station. Then, when she moved back to Mystique, she got her heart set on an old home that she just had to buy. She's been saving up for it for years."

"What happened?"

"You've said enough, Immy. Drop it." Rayne nudged her friend, then shot her piercing gaze to Clark. "That's all you need to know. If you really care about Gabby, and I think you do, then you should be as open and honest about your feelings and your past with her. Once she feels you're being upfront, she'll tell you the rest herself."

"No, Rayne, Immy's right—he needs to know." The librarian pointed a fork at him. "You bought her dream house."

Oh, no. That explained the tears in her eyes when he invited her in. Her funny expressions on their date when he talked about improvements. "I didn't know."

"You couldn't have." Imogene's smile was sincere. "And deep down inside, Gab knows that."

"I would have never bought the house she wanted if I'd known."

"Hard to know with a Yankee." But Sheldon flashed him a wide smile.

"You know, you should talk to Gabby. Soon," Rayne said with a nod. "No sense waiting. Lay your intentions out on the table. She'll appreciate your candor and honesty."

He choked on his coffee. "She's at work." He glanced at his watch. "Or will be soon."

"Yes." Sheldon quirked a single brow up. "And you have a problem with that? Aren't you her boss?"

They were trying to help him? They'd given him approval? Elation pushed his hunger even further away.

"They're right. You should go as soon as you finish eating," Imogene nearly whispered. "Tell her how you feel."

Swallowing, he nodded. "I will."

Her eyes widened.

Clark stood in the hall of the station, his hands cupped around his face, pressing against the glass to the studio to stare at Gabby.

Gabby motioned him inside. "What're you doing here?" Her tone was as soft as the rain flittering to the ground following the hard storm of earlier as he eased into the studio and took the seat in front of her. "Has something else happened?"

"No, nothing like that. I just wanted to see you. Talk to you." He blinked, his heart racing.

Those eyes of hers…man, he could drown in the liquid emotions expressed in them. He'd swear he could see forever lurking there.

"Clark?"

Jerking back from fantasyland, he forced a smile. "I wanted to talk to you. About my house."

Her expression went void. "I only have a minute left before I'm back on air."

He opened his mouth, but she shook a finger at him while adjusting the headset over her ears.

"This is Gabby Rogillio, and welcome to dedications on KLUV. Up next is a special dedication going out to Casey from Robin. She says she loves you with all her heart. Love to you all, Mystique." She pushed the button to start the song, and then shoved the headset down to hang around her neck. She stared at Clark. "Would you like a cup of coffee? I just made a fresh pot."

He shook his head. "I just had dinner—I mean, supper."

She smiled weakly as she doodled on her desktop. "So, what about your house?"

Clark shifted in his seat, the old chair creaking in protest. "I didn't know it was the house you wanted. I would never have bought it had I known you were saving up for it."

"You couldn't have known." She tossed him another smile, but it still didn't reach her eyes.

"Well, I just wanted you to know that…" He clenched and unclenched his hands. "I just want you to know that I had no idea."

"Just a minute, time to queue up a few more dedications. Hold that thought." Gabby settled the earpieces snugly over her ears.

Once she'd aired the dedications and started the song, she pushed down the headset again. "Have you heard anything else? About the case?"

"Nothing. You?"

"Well, I talked with Eric about Mr. Tankersly. He said his stepfather was abusive."

Clark nodded. "Fits with the rage we saw in him during our altercation."

"It's just…" Gabby shrugged and chewed on her bottom lip.

"Just what?"

"I found something tonight that bugs me a little."

"Such as?" He leaned forward, resting his elbows against the small desk.

She worried her bottom lip with her teeth. "A deposit slip from Eric's personal account. For quite a bit of money."

"Exactly how much money?"

"Fifty thousand dollars."

He let out a low whistle and leaned back. Fifty thousand dollars? "Dated recently?"

She nodded, her eyes asking the questions her voice wouldn't.

"Any idea where he'd get that kind of money?"

"None." She clicked the pen. *Click-click-click.* "It does look strange."

Click. Click.

"Did you ask him about it?"

"He'd already left."

"I have a friend from…older times, and I can ask him to look into it." He ran a hand over the uninjured side of his face, studying her. "Gabby, why don't you trust me?"

"I do." No hesitation.

But she still wasn't being completely forthcoming. He shook his head as his pulse pounded against his skull. "Not in business you don't. Why?"

Click. Click. Click.

"It's not that I don't trust you, Clark…"

The silence filled the room like dead airtime.

"You don't. Every single time I even mention my past business or the station, you close up as tight as a clam."

She dropped the pen onto the desk, shoved the headset over her head, and then punched the button to broadcast the dedications she read from her sheet. After queuing the song, she stared across the desk at him. "I just got burned before by newshounds, okay? Let's just leave it at that."

"No, I don't want to leave it at that." His voice came out as unyielding as her expression. He swallowed, then softened his tone. "I want you to trust me, Gabby."

"Why is this so important to you?"

"Because you're important to me."

"You hardly know me." Her words were barely a whisper.

"And that's part of the problem. I want to get to know you better." She chewed her bottom lip, not responding.

"Gabby, I don't want to frighten you off. I think you know

there's something simmering between us." He laid his hand over hers. "That kiss…" Had nearly scorched him. Hadn't she felt it?

The heat from the contact sent little beads of perspiration to the back of his neck. No sense stopping now—might as well get it all out in the open. "But we've got to be open and honest in order to get to know each other better. I want that. Do you?"

She licked her lips, but remained as unmovable as the Confederate monument outside Mystique's courthouse square.

"I think we have a chance at something here. Something wonderful and lasting." He withdrew his hand, letting it fall into his lap.

"Clark—"

"No, let me finish." He gulped in air. "You interest me in a way no other woman has, Gabby Rogillio, and I have no intention of letting that drop without getting to know you better." He stood, towering over her. "You think about that. In the meantime, I'll have an investigator look into Eric's accounts and into Martin and his late wife and see what I can dig up."

Her jaw hung slack, but her stare stayed glued to his.

"How about we meet for lunch tomorrow? Give you some time alone to think about what I've said." He took a step backward. "Say about eleven at Ms. Minnie's?"

She nodded.

"I'll see you then." He turned to head to the studio door, then stopped. Glancing over his shoulder, he stared at her.

In four strides, he'd crossed the room to her. He gripped her shoulders and pulled her up to him. With the slightest pressure from the tip of his finger, Clark lifted her chin, then lowered his lips to hers.

Her lips were soft and yielding, spinning his mind and emotions into an eddy.

He ended the kiss way before he was ready for it to be over, and withdrew from her in just a fraction of a heartbeat. "I'll see you tomorrow," he whispered, his breath teasing her cheek.

Gabby sank back into the chair.

He resisted the urge to whistle as he left the studio.

In the dark parking lot, he slipped into the rental car. A breeze skipped across the open space. Would she even show up for lunch tomorrow? *Lord, please let her show up.*

Driving home, he listened to the dedications on KLUV. He didn't hear Gabby's exact words, just listened to the throaty smoothness of her one-of-a-kind voice gliding under his skin and tangoing into his heart.

He'd told her the truth…he did want to get to know her better. His interest and attraction held his throat so tight he couldn't swallow.

Once in the house, Clark glanced around at the renovations he'd already started. To Gabby's house. Oh, she'd downplayed how important this house was to her, but he could tell Gabby loved the house. How had he missed that before? As he looked around, he could imagine her here, in this house. With him.

The knot in his throat cinched. After Philly, he didn't believe in happily-ever-after. Yet, here he was, dreaming of a perfect ending with a woman who still seemed unsure whether or not she could trust him.

He glanced at the clock. It was late, but not so much so that he thought he'd wake his former reporter. Clark flipped open his cell and punched in the man's number.

"Yes?"

"It's Clark. I'm sorry for calling so late."

"No worries, dude. What can I do for you?"

"I need you to find out some information for me. Personal information about some people here in Mystique." He'd set the hound on the trail of the fox now. Let the games begin.

SEVENTEEN

Rushing across KLUV's parking lot, her heels slipping against loose gravel, Gabby noticed Robert's car in its usual spot, and her breath caught. Had Robert woken up? She shoved open the double doors and crossed into the reception foyer.

Loud voices echoed off the normally serene walls. Eric's deep baritone vibrated throughout the station, followed by a woman's sobs. Gabby strode toward Eric's office. Although the door was closed, she didn't bother to knock before entering.

Eric stood behind his desk, his hair sticking up and gaze darting over the seated woman's hunched form.

Amber, with sobs shaking her body, was speaking. "You can't ask me to—" Her words died as her glance shot to Gabby.

The look in the woman's stare froze Gabby to the core. Remorse, anger and perhaps fear soaked her tear-filled eyes. But there was something more lurking behind those irises…a true sign to Amber Ellison's mental state—brokenness. Gabby should know—she'd seen it in her own reflection after Blake Riggsdale had finished with her.

Dropping into the chair beside Amber, Gabby threw an arm around the other woman's shoulders. "Amber, what is it? Has something happened with Robert?"

She sniffled and shrugged off Gabby's arm before jumping

to her feet. "I just can't do this. Not now. Not here. Not…" Her glance moved to Eric's, where it lingered for a moment before she jerked her stare back to Gabby. "I just can't. I'm sorry." Without another word, she fled from the room.

Gabby stood.

"Just let her go." Eric's quiet words halted her.

"What were you two arguing about?"

His face flushed a brighter red. "Nothing. She's just emotional."

"No, I heard you yelling when I came in. What about?" Gabby crossed her arms.

For a split second, anger slipped across his features. In a blink of an eye, it was gone again. Had she imagined it? "She just refuses to pick up Robert's personal stuff. That's what I'd asked her to do. For Mr. McKay."

Suspicions receded partially. Gabby remained wary as she dropped her hands to the desk. "Oh." She glanced at the computer screen behind him. "Is there a problem with payroll?"

He spun around and clicked on the computer keyboard. "Trying to figure things out. I think Robert might've been embezzling money."

"What? You're mistaken." Robert wouldn't embezzle money. No way.

"Well, Robert made three different large withdrawals over the past six months." His fingers flew over the keys. "One for fifty thousand dollars and two for twenty-five."

She sank back into the chair, rubbing her chin. Why would Robert take out so much money? They hadn't bought anything new for the station in years. "Maybe he used that money to buy back Howard's shares of the station?"

"I don't think so. Deposits were made regularly every month into the account. The only checks drawn out each month were legit—payroll, advertising and the like. Then, six months ago, a cash withdrawal was made on the account, followed by the other two."

It didn't make sense. "What was the balance in the account before the cash withdrawals began?"

"Fifty-six thousand and some change." He rolled his shoulders, his bones popping.

"On average, what was the running balance in the account before these withdrawals?"

The clicks came faster, and louder. Or maybe that was just her perception.

"Between fifty and sixty thousand. Deposits were made regularly, as they should, but once the balance hit near the sixty-thousand mark, the withdrawal hit. Then the balance would go back up with deposits." He sighed. "And another withdrawal would put the balance back below ten thousand."

Nothing added up.

Eric let out a long sigh, laced his fingers behind his head, and stared at her. "See what I mean? The only thing that makes sense is embezzlement. And who could it be but Robert?"

"I don't know." *Think, Gabby, think.* There was a piece of the puzzle right here—just out of her grasp. What wasn't she seeing?

Her cell phone chirped. She dug into her purse for it. "Hello."

"Are you standing me up?"

Her heart faltered at the sound of his voice. "Clark."

"The one and only. I'm sitting here at Ms. Minnie's."

She checked her watch—11:22. "I'm sorry. I lost track of time." She cut her gaze to Eric, who made shooing motions. "I'm on my way now. Be there in five."

Gabby slammed the phone closed and slipped it into her purse. "We'll talk tomorrow." She moved toward the door.

"Sure you don't want to work tonight?" His tone had shifted

to light and teasing. "I'm sure Harry would enjoy the break." Harry, a part-time deejay, filled in on the regulars' days off.

"My one day off? Are you kidding?" She hitched her purse strap over her shoulder. "I have a lunch date. Later."

His laughter followed her out of the station, into the parking lot and inside her car. She wanted to take comfort in it, but couldn't. Eric was her friend, she trusted him, and yet…was it really just a coincidence that the deposit slip she'd found matched one of the withdrawals from the station's accounts?

She headed toward where Clark sat at a table near the window, her steps light.

"Sorry I'm late." Her words came out in a burst as she dropped into the seat across from him.

"No problem."

Ms. Minnie ambled up. "Hi there, Gabby. What can I get y'all?"

"What's today's special? It smells divine."

"I made some crawfish étouffée fresh this morning."

"That's what I'll have."

Clark smiled at the diner owner. "Make that two, Ms. Minnie."

"Iced tea?"

After agreeing to the drink, he waited until the proprietor had left to readdress Gabby.

"So, guess what I found out."

Oh, so it was serious time already. She swallowed the knot of fear. "What?"

"Aunt Beulah was right. Amber Ellison, back then Stevens, did have a baby out of wedlock the summer after her high school graduation."

Her heart began to beat in double time. "What else?"

"Amber Stevens gave birth to a healthy, bouncing baby boy in September at Children's Hospital in New Orleans, Louisiana."

"Oh my." She ran a finger over her bottom lip. "What happened to the baby?"

"Here's where it gets tricky. The baby was adopted by a Paul and Jane, no last name. It's listed as a closed adoption, so no further information is available."

Ms. Minnie chose that moment to deliver their savory and aromatic bowls. "Here ya go. If you need anything else, just holler."

They quickly offered up grace and then Clark grabbed a piece of garlic bread.

"But that's it? A dead end?" She leaned back in the booth, the vinyl squeaking. "I don't even know why it's important, but I just feel that it is. And now to have hit a roadblock."

"I said the adoption was closed. I didn't say my source gave up digging."

Did this mean there could be evidence of a connection? "So there could be more?"

He smiled as he dipped the tip of his bread into the thick souplike meal. "I told him to keep looking until he'd found everything possible."

Gabby smiled and lifted a spoon to her mouth. The sharp and stinging spices warmed her mouth, exploding in a melody of bite and flavor.

After breaking his bread in half, Clark slipped a bite into his mouth.

Her stare shot to his mouth…the strong jawline…the perfect symmetry of his features. He was a beautiful specimen of a healthy, red-blooded male. Gabby's stomach rumbled as she brought her analysis to a screeching halt. His unpretentious speech from last night still rang in her ears.

"So, did you think about what I said last night?" Was he a mind reader, too?

She set down her spoon, lifted her glass and took a long, slow sip. Anything to stall this conversation.

"Gabby?" His eyes were so open, so honest.

"I did." She set her glass down with a shaking hand. Tea sloshed over the side and onto her hand. Just what she needed to cool off. "I won't lie to you, Clark. I'm very interested in you."

"Uh-oh, I hear a *but* in there." He steepled his hands over his bowl.

She gave a little chuckle. "But I don't know if I want to risk becoming involved with you or anyone right now."

"Why?"

"Because…" Why didn't she want to take a chance? She deserved to be happy, to have love.

"Because why?" He rested his chin on his interwoven fingers, peering across the table at her with those piercing eyes of his.

She fisted her hands in her lap, then jerked them and laid her palms flat on the table.

"You were hurt before. Tell me." His voice was smooth, as if coaxing a kitten down from a tree.

Could she trust him? With her heart? She studied his face, his eyes… Was he as sincere as he appeared, as he sounded?

He laid a hand over hers. Warmth filled her.

Whether or not she trusted him, she owed him the truth. He'd shared his past with her.

She took a deep breath. "In college, I was interning at a local news station. Reporting." She smiled at him, hoping it didn't look as wobbly as it felt.

"The station manager, and son of the owner, befriended me." The memory of Blake's attention still haunted her. "We actually began dating." She took in another deep breath.

Clark squeezed her hand, his smile brightening her dark recollections.

"Then, some college girls began being stalked. On campus, at their apartments, at jobs. Letters, pictures, phone calls—things that weren't exactly harmful, just frightening." Gabby paused, the memory washing over her. "Of course the news station ran a special feature on the issue. I was the reporter.

"My boyfriend, Blake, encouraged me to be visual in my reporting. To make the public aware, he swore to me." She ran a hand through her hair, wishing she could whisk away the past as easily.

"What happened?" Clark's hand released hers.

"Oh, I did all the reports. I mean, I was informing the public, helping these young women be smart, right?" Gabby took a sip of her tea, then stared into the cloudy liquid.

"The station's ratings soared. But that was it. I'd done my job." She shrugged. "Blake wanted more. He encouraged me to provoke the stalker. To try and annoy him publicly. To get him to make a mistake, at least that's what Blake said."

An icy finger traced her spine. "And me being the naive and trusting person I was then, I did it. I deliberately set out to enrage a stalker."

"Oh, Gabby."

"It gets even better." She tossed a caustic smile across the table. "Without warning me, Blake concluded my segment with a couple of personal details about me. Just enough information that the stalker could find me."

"Oh, no." Clark's eyes darkened a shade.

"Oh, yes. At first I was livid, but Blake told me how great the ratings were, how I was coming to his father's attention, how this could make my career in broadcast journalism." She shook her head, dismay pounding against her temples. "I bought into it. Hook, line and sinker. All of it."

He interlaced his fingers with hers, warming the chill from her.

"Blake went even further. He'd planned for the stalker to

come after me, and he kept me under close observation, with a camera crew no less." Gabby dusted imaginary crumbs from the table. "All without me knowing."

"What happened?"

"Just what Blake had wanted. The stalker came after me. Upped his actions from his previous victims. No cards or pictures or calls for me. No, he came after me physically. Caught me in a parking lot. Grabbed me, threw me against the hood of my own car." Tears erupted from her eyes, but she didn't blink them back. She'd come this far, and now she couldn't stop the release of water over the dam even if she tried.

For good, bad or indifferent, Clark McKay was going to hear the whole sordid ordeal.

She sniffed, but kept her attention focused on her glass. "The stalker spit in my face, called me horrible names and threatened to show me just how much of a *coward* he wasn't. And my knight in shining armor, the one who wanted this to happen and was supposed to save me? He sat back and recorded the incident. He let this man humiliate and terrify me so he could air it."

"What happened?" Clark's voice came out heavy. "What'd this stalker do to you?"

"Well, after the yelling and spitting, he ripped my shirt." She closed her eyes, her words coming in bursts. "Blake, I suppose, figured that was enough. He came rushing on the scene—the cameras still rolling, of course—to be my hero." She opened her eyes and stared at Clark. "And he succeeded—the ratings for that airing went through the roof."

"But what about you?"

She slapped the tears from her face. "I survived. I learned my lesson—that ratings are the most important thing. Made the decision that if that's the way the business worked, I didn't want to be a party to it." Gabby let out a long breath, not as broken and harsh as before. "I switched majors, went into communications. And here I am."

Did he have a clue how much it had cost her to tell him all this, relive such a painful event?

Clark slipped from the seat and moved around the table. He knelt beside her, staring into her eyes. "I'm sorry that happened to you, Gabby." He wrapped his arms around her, tugging her to him. "And I'll never hurt you like that. Ever."

He lifted his lips to hers, softly brushing against them. Her heart pounded so hard he must be able to feel it against his chest. He deepened the kiss, burying his hands in her hair. She liked the feeling of security and acceptance she found in his embrace.

Most of all, she liked the way her heart lifted as he kissed her.

Clark fought against holding Gabby tighter, afraid to scare her off. He ran a thumb against her chin, wanting to take away all the pain she'd endured.

The acid ate at his stomach lining as he reflected on what she had shared. This ex-boyfriend was below disgusting, beyond selfish. The urge to hit someone hard—this Blake person in particular—had Clark tightening the muscles in his biceps. But Gabby needed him, needed him to understand her past.

He cuddled her closer, to where he could feel her heartbeat against his chest. No, he'd never hurt her. All he wanted was to keep her exactly as close and exactly as safe as she was at that moment.

Somehow, the idea of a life with Gabby Rogillio didn't scare him, didn't make him want to pack up and run back home. Just the opposite. He wanted to share his life with her, and hers with him. But as he held her and rested his chin against her head, he knew he had to take it very slow. She'd been hurt so badly before.

He'd tread carefully with her heart. But one day, it would belong to him and him alone.

EIGHTEEN

Hair was a messy thing. Gross, if one really thought about it.

Gabby watched Tonna sweep up stray bits of hair. She'd brought Clark with her to meet the girls at Tonna's Tresses and bring everyone up to speed on what Gabby and Clark had discovered. Gabby's mind still drifted to him and their agreement to give the romance between them a fair shot. She smiled at him from across the room.

"So, how does this illegitimate child of Amber's play into everything?" Rayne studied her perfectly manicured nails.

"We don't know yet." Gabby fought back the sneeze. "I'm wondering if Sam knows anything."

Clark moved to stand behind Gabby. "He didn't say anything to us the other morning."

"But wasn't he drunker than Cooter Brown?" Immy straightened the pens in the cup beside the appointment book. "I mean, he could have omitted details."

"True." Gabby folded the last clean cape and set the stack on the shelf. "Maybe Sam knows what happened to the baby."

"Again, this is important why?" Rayne glanced out the window. "I just don't see how it connects."

"It's like a really big puzzle with lots of missing pieces, that's for sure." Gabby moved toward the stack of clean towels. An idea smacked her across the face. "Y'all, what if… Now play along with me for a minute here, but just what if that's why Robert and Amber were having marital problems—he found out about the baby?"

"Good point." Tonna swept the hair into the dustpan. "Unless Amber told him before they got married."

"Wouldn't she have?" Sheldon slicked lipstick over her lips and popped them together. "I mean, they got married pretty quickly after she would have had the baby. She'd have been still pudgy and stuff."

"Oh, for pity's sake, Sheldon. She was young. She probably popped the baby out and got her figure back the next day." Tonna shoved the broom into the storage closet. "I see plenty of younger women in here who do that. Makes me sick." She shook her head, her wild auburn curls flying around her shoulders. "My luck, when I finally settle down and have a baby, I'll still be carrying around baby fat when the kid starts college."

Clark gave a laugh.

"So, what now?" Immy asked, always the peacemaker.

"To be honest," Gabby said, folding the towel and setting it atop the stack, "we really want to do a little investigating. We need to put the pieces together, figure out what's what."

"And you plan to do that how?" Rayne crossed her arms over her chest. Even the defensive pose looked model-perfect when she executed it.

"We want to talk to Sam, Amber and maybe even Martin Tankersly." Clark squeezed Gabby's shoulders.

"You know, this is like one of those mysteries we got in not too long ago at the library," Sheldon said as she leaned on the counter. "See, what happened was this couple's house was broken into, and the local constable didn't have a clue who the—"

Tonna snapped her fingers in front of Sheldon's face. "This

isn't some novel, this is important." She turned to face Gabby and Clark. "I think that's a great idea. Count me in."

"Shouldn't we leave this to Sheriff McGruder?" Immy's expression matched her tone. "I mean, he *is* the law enforcer in town."

Sheldon's laugh came out as a snort. "Please. That man would have trouble finding his hand in the dark with a flashlight."

"What is it about him that rubs you raw? I mean, we all agree he isn't the brightest bulb in the light fixture, but you make it sound almost personal." Tonna shoved Sheldon's arm. "Why the sudden sarcasm toward him, sistah?"

Cheeks flaming, Sheldon pushed Tonna's arm back. "I'm not being sarcastic about him."

"Oh, yes, you are."

"You most certainly are."

"Oh, come on. You're being downright snippy toward him."

She held up her hands. "Okay, okay." Sheldon tossed her head. "We went out a couple of weeks ago."

"What? When?" Gabby asked for the entire group.

"Just a couple of weekends ago. It was nothing big, just supper at Steamboat Annie's."

"What happened?" Despite her keen interest, Rayne's posture never slipped from pageant-perfect.

"I thought we had a nice time. He kissed my hand goodbye and told me he'd call me." Sheldon let out a long sigh. "I haven't heard from him since."

"He's been a bit busy with the murder investigation, Sheldon," Clark volunteered.

"Maybe, but he could have still picked up the phone and called me. Oh, well. You know, we actually went to our high school prom together. I thought we would start dating, but then I went on to college."

"Oh, that's so sweet," Immy practically gushed.

"Obviously it's not going to happen, Immy. Don't go getting all Hallmark-y on me."

Clark's admission that he'd been scared to approach her, but more scared not to, flashed through Gabby's memory. "Maybe he's scared."

Leaning down, Clark planted a kiss on her temple. Heat burned Gabby's face as Sheldon whipped around. "Scared? Of what? He's a big sheriff, not afraid of anything."

Clark shrugged. "Maybe he's scared of what he's feeling for you."

"Oh, please. This isn't a daytime soap. The man blew me off, plain and simple." Sheldon straightened her shoulders. "So, let's go visit Sam."

"Are you sure you want to?" Gabby stared at each of her best friends, one at a time. Each nodded. "Alrighty then, let's roll."

Gabby whipped her SUV into Sam's driveway, parking behind his old Ford pickup truck.

"What're you going to say, Gab?" Immy blinked those caring eyes of hers.

All the nice phrases she'd mentally rehearsed on the drive over flew out of Gabby's brain. "I really don't know. Guess I'll just play it by ear."

"You can't just go in and try to pry details about this man's painful past without an idea how to do it." Tonna clicked off her seat belt. "Even I wouldn't do that."

Gabby opened her door. "Well, I'll be tactful, for goodness sakes." She stepped onto the loose gravel, then slammed the door behind her. She made her way up the stairs. The *bam! bam! bam!* of the other truck doors shutting let her know the others were right behind her. Clark wove his fingers with hers.

Gabby jumped when the door opened with a loud creak.

"Ms. Gabby, what brings you here this evening?" Sam's eyes were bloodshot as he glanced over her shoulder. "Ladies and Mr. McKay."

"We need to talk to you, Mr. Sam. It's important."

He let out a grunt. The stench of stale liquor on his breath nearly gagged Gabby. "What about?"

She licked her lips. "Amber Ellison."

His eyes clouded, then cleared. He pushed the door open all the way. "Well, then, come on in." He moved his large frame from blocking the threshold.

Gabby perched on the edge of the couch as her friends took seats from the limited selection. Clark remained behind her, strong as a statue, but just his presence offered her comfort and strength.

Staleness hung in the air. A layer of dust coated the coffee table and the hunting magazines resting on top, making her want to sneeze. She curled her hands in her lap to resist the urge to fling open the living-room windows, just to let in a breath of fresh air.

Sam hunkered down on the battered leather recliner. A puff of dust surrounded him in the setting sun sprinkling in from the dingy curtains. "So, whatcha want to know about Amber?"

"You told me and Clark the other day that you and she were high school sweethearts, but then she left right after graduation." Maybe he'd pick up the conversation ball now.

"Yep."

"Mr. Sam, we already know she left because she was pregnant. Did her parents send her away and make her give the baby up for adoption?"

His face lost all expression, save for his eyes. They filled with tears and confusion. "What did you say?"

Gabby swallowed, hard.

Immy, bless her heart, moved to sit beside Sam and took his hand in hers. "So, you didn't know she was pregnant when she left town?"

"P-pregnant? Amber?" He shook his head. "No, that can't be. She would have told me."

Immy glared at Gabby, making her squirm. Had he really not known? Could Amber have been so cold as to not tell him?

"I know this is hard, Mr. Sam." Immy put an arm around the man, still clutching his hand with her free one. "But it's been confirmed. Amber did have a baby that September."

Tears pooled in his eyes. "Of course it's possible. I mean, we'd been…you know, together. But why wouldn't she have told me?"

Too bad Gabby didn't have any answers. "I don't know, Mr. Sam. I'm sorry. I thought you knew."

"That explains a lot." He sniffed. "I mean, she left so suddenly and wouldn't tell me where she was going."

Sheldon leaned forward. "Had y'all been arguing?"

"Well, I can't rightly recall." He ran a hand over his thinning hair. "I remember her parents weren't too happy about how close we were. They wanted her to go to college and get away from Mystique."

"She just left without saying goodbye?" Tonna's eyes brimmed with tears.

He rested his elbows on his knees. "She told me she was going to visit some relatives. That's it. She never said nothing about being pregnant." He closed his eyes and hung his head.

Immy absently straightened the throw pillows. "You couldn't have known, Mr. Sam."

"The b-baby." He lifted his gaze to settle on Gabby. "You said she gave it up for adoption. She had it?"

"From what we've learned, she had the baby at Children's Hospital in New Orleans. He was adopted by a Paul and Jane, no last names."

"He? She had a boy?"

"Yes." Gabby's voice croaked as she realized what he must be thinking. Her heart ripped in two.

"A son. I have a son." His voice trailed off as he shook his head. "I can't believe she never told me." He jumped to his feet, startling the girls. "I have a son. I have to find him."

"Mr. Sam," Clark began, "I have someone looking into the adoption. We don't even know the last name of the people who adopted the child."

"My son. Someone adopted my son." His big frame trembled. "The son Amber never told me I had." His eyes turned wild.

This was going from bad to worse quicker than a sand castle being washed away by waves. She had to do something—anything—to calm him down. Gabby stood and took hold of his arm. "Mr. Sam, let us find out what we can for you." She tugged on his arm until his stare focused on her face. "I promise you, as soon as we find out anything, I'll let you know."

The tears fell from his eyes, dripping down his stubbly face. "She knew how much I wanted a family." His eyes sought out Gabby's. "Why didn't she tell me?"

Her mouth suddenly felt as parched as the desert. "I don't know, Mr. Sam. I don't know."

But she fully intended to find out.

The phone on Clark's belt rang, nearly causing him to jump out of his skin. "McKay."

"It's me."

"Oh, hi." Clark excused himself from Sam Wood's living room, anxious to talk to his source in private. "Have you found out anything?"

"Yes, sir, I sure did. I found out the last name of the adoptive parents."

A long pause preceded a crackle over the line. Was the man going to make him pull the information from him? "Well?"

"Masters. A Paul and Jane Masters."

Masters…Masters…Clark knew that name. From where? He ran through the filing cabinets of his mind, pulling out data sheets on people he'd met since coming to Mystique. Masters. Finally, he had it. "Was the child named Eric?"

"I'm working on finding out."

A sick sensation swept across his gut. "I know an Eric Masters."

"Did you know that Paul Masters died when the child was only three?"

"No." What was the connection? What was he missing here? "I want you to keep checking and see if the widow Jane remarried. Specifically, if she remarried a man named Martin Tankersly. And find out if the child's name was Eric."

"I'm on it."

Clark hung up the phone. He didn't move.

Amber Ellison and Sam Wood had had a baby. That baby was given up for adoption. The people who adopted the baby were Paul and Jane Masters. Eric Masters was KLUV's station manager, and worked closely with Gabby. What was the connection? It was there, Clark could feel it.

Maybe Gabby could make sense of it all. She certainly made his life make sense lately. For a change—a very refreshing and welcome change.

Gabby and her friends joined him on the porch, closing the door behind them.

"I'll check on him tomorrow," Imogene said.

"Who was that on the phone?" Gabby asked.

"I just heard back from my source."

"And?"

"The baby was adopted by Paul and Jane Masters."

NINETEEN

Gabby remained silent on the drive from Sam's to Martin Tankersly's house. Immy had gently scolded her for just blurting out the truth to Sam, and remorse shifted Gabby's movements into slow motion.

Now she had to wonder about what Clark's sources had found out. Was Eric the child Amber had? When would all the confusion, deceptions and secrets end?

"I know you didn't mean any ill will, Gab, but maybe you ought to plan what you're gonna say before you talk to Martin." Sheldon's words held no malice.

"I'm working on it. Ever since I heard what Mr. Tankersly yelled about an adopted son, I've wondered what it meant." What was she missing? The elusive link which would put the whole chain together was right there…bobbing just out of her reach.

"Considering the fight you and Martin had, Clark, I'm wondering if maybe it'd be best for you to stay in the truck while we talk to him," Immy said.

Gabby cut her gaze to Clark. "Probably not a bad idea."

"Fine. I'll stay in the truck. Unless he makes a wrong move."

He worried about her! How nice. It'd been a long time since a man had worried about her, save her papa and Antonio.

Rayne tapped her perfectly manicured fingernail against her

front teeth, not smudging her glossy lipstick. "I'm not under-standing how all this is connected. I mean, yeah, Mr. Sam was upset because he feels like Robert took Amber away from him, but let's be honest—I just don't see him murdering Howard. There's no logic there."

"Unless he shot Howard thinking it was Robert?" Tonna interrupted.

"What if he recently found out about the baby Amber gave up and wanted Robert out of the picture? Maybe so he and Amber could have another chance?" Gabby knew it was a big reach, but she didn't have another plausible reason to suspect Sam. Truth be told, she had a gut feeling that Sam wasn't involved at all. But lost love was a strong motive.

"Great day in the morning, Gabby. That man had no clue he had fathered a child until you said something. You could see the surprise and pain in his eyes, plain as day." Immy's words were as harsh as a schoolmarm's. "He was plum shocked, that's what he was."

"I'm sure he'll be just fine, Immy." Tonna gave a little snort. "People get shocks every day of the week and they survive."

"But he'd been drinking the other day, and from the smell of things just now, I'd say he's still nipping at the bottle. I'm a little concerned about him."

Tonna shrugged. "Then check on him later, if it'll make you feel better."

"I'd like to know what happened to the baby," Sheldon whispered from the backseat. "I mean, was Amber kept up to date on the baby's progress like some adoptions? I saw a special on *Oprah* about it."

"I doubt it." Gabby turned the vehicle onto the street where Mr. Tankersly lived. "According to the listed information, it was a closed adoption—the adoptive parents didn't even list their last name."

"True." Rayne nodded. "But we now know what it is? How does this involve Martin?"

"I haven't a clue. There's just so much that points to him. He's Eric's stepfather and from what Eric told me, he was abusive. Him showing up at the station the other night and getting into it with Clark..." Gabby pulled the SUV into the driveway. "Here we are."

Before they could exit the vehicle, Mr. Tankersly stormed out of the house and down the porch steps. Funny how Gabby had never considered the man's build before—he looked like Ichabod Crane, with his long skinny legs and arms sticking out from a slight torso.

"Stay here," she said to Clark before opening her door. "Mr. Tankersly, may I speak to you?" Gabby rushed to meet him before he got into his beat-up car. Her friends followed in her wake.

"What do *you* want?" he all but snarled at her. A shining bruise decorated one side of his nose, and the split in his lip boasted a thick scab.

"I just want to talk to you. About your wife."

He ceased walking. His entire body stiffened. "What about her?"

"I heard you say something about your wife having an adopted son." Her blood seemed to pump faster through her system, giving her energy she knew she shouldn't have. "I didn't know she had a son. Well, other than Eric."

Martin's laughter, callous and hard, rang out. "Why would I tell you anything?"

"I'm just trying to find out who's behind Howard's murder."

"Again, why would I care? KLUV is my rival, even though it's not been much of a competitive force lately. Besides, what's any of this got to do with Jane?"

Gabby stood mute.

"Actually, Mr. Tankersly—" Rayne moved to stand just slightly in front of Gabby "—I was interested, too. You know, because of my daddy's B and B being so close to KLUV and not knowing if Robert's really the killer." She batted her eyelashes at the older man. "He'd hate to think the violence could shift over to our place. A murder…" She shivered, then hugged herself. Those big eyes stared at him.

The expression in the man's eyes was clear—the VanDoren name carried weight. Old money, old power. And Charles VanDoren exuded both. Martin Tankersly had the good sense not to offend a VanDoren. Any VanDoren.

"Well, now, Rayne honey, I don't know what I can tell you." His face softened, the leathery wrinkles easing a smidgen. "I don't know anything about that murder." His gaze raked over Gabby. "No matter what others might be saying."

Shifting from one foot to the other, Gabby stared at Rayne.

"No one's accusing you of anything, Mr. Tankersly," Rayne said in her softest voice. "We're just trying to figure things out." She batted her lashes again while hugging herself. "To feel safe and all."

"Well now, I can understand your concern, ladies—" he even included Gabby in his gaze "—but I don't think y'all have anything to worry about." Now his stare locked on Gabby's, sending the strangest sense of foreboding shooting down her legs. "And now that Robert's been arrested, there's been no more signs of violence. Right?"

Gabby swallowed back her retort. What about her slashed tires and threatening note and phone call? Or his and Clark's odd altercation in the parking lot? And the sheriff never did tell her why Mr. Tankersly was at the station to begin with.

"And it's the first murder we've had in Mystique in decades." He shook his head. "No, I think you ladies can rest assured that everything is just fine now."

"Amber Ellison said you'd been underpricing advertising, cutting KLUV's business," Sheldon piped up.

The smile dropped quickly as he narrowed his eyes and shot a frigid stare at the town librarian. "Just because I can afford to run advertising specials doesn't mean I'm doing anything wrong, young lady."

"Of course not," Rayne practically cooed. "She didn't mean anything by that. We're just curious."

He smiled at her. "You know, used to be Robert was a worthy business adversary. We'd try to outbid each other on advertising spots, run specials to lure away sponsors, things like that. But then that worthless stepson of mine went to work for KLUV and filled Robert's head with all kinds of lies about me." He flexed his skinny arms.

"Mr. Tankersly," Rayne drew his attention with her sugary voice, "I heard you told Clark that your stepson was adopted."

He snorted. "I never *told* that Yankee anything. But I did say that Jane and her first husband were unable to have children. They adopted a son from some relative of hers that got knocked up in her teens. And that son is Eric."

Gabby stood ramrod-stiff, her muscles refusing to budge.

So Eric *was* the adopted baby. Another piece of the puzzle had fallen into place.

A gust of wind tiptoed across the air, scattering lavender petals from a nearby wisteria bush. Through the open window, the warm smell of freshly cut grass filled the car's cabin.

Gabby dragged her steps back to the SUV, the other girls already at the vehicle. She opened the driver's door and slipped behind the wheel.

Tonna let out a shallow gasp. "I can't believe it. Eric, adopted. I wonder if he even knows."

Clark clicked his seat belt into place. "Tankersly confirmed it?"

Gabby turned onto Shannon Street. "He did."

"My source called back while you were out of the car," Clark said.

"And? Don't keep us in suspense." Sheldon playfully slapped his shoulder.

"Did you guys know that it was Amber's cousin and her husband who adopted Eric?"

You guys? Man, she'd have to work on polishing the Yankee out of him. Gabby started to chuckle when the facts slammed against her brain. "If a family member adopted a child, why the closed adoption?"

"From what I understand, that's fairly common. It's to protect the birth mother. How would you like to find out your aunt Edna is really your mom?" His voice hummed with excitement.

"I see your point," Immy stated.

Clark continued, "Most all relative adoptions are closed. As are the majority of stranger adoptions. Rumor has it that it makes the process easier all around."

"I guess." Gabby slowed for a stop sign.

She drummed her fingers against the steering wheel as she lost herself in thought. Amber Ellison had left town when she found out she was pregnant by Sam Wood. She went to Louisiana, had a baby boy. A cousin of hers adopted the baby. She met Robert some way, fell in love, married him and returned to Mystique. Her adopted son, years later, showed up in town.

Rayne broke the silence, repeating the question Tonna had voiced and Gabby had swimming around in her mind. "Gabby, do you think Eric knows he was adopted?"

"I don't know. He's never mentioned it." But wouldn't that be something Mr. Tankersly would have thrown in his face time and again? Gabby hauled in a deep breath as she turned the SUV toward Main Street. "If he knew, has he figured out who his mother is? How would that make him feel?"

"Probably rotten," Sheldon quipped. "But how does this fact play into the murder?"

That was a question Gabby couldn't answer. "There has to be more. Has to be a connection of some sort, one we haven't made yet."

For once, not one of the them had an opinion to voice.

What didn't they know? There was a missing piece of the puzzle left. The one piece that would make the picture come into focus. But what? Gabby hit the side of her fist against the steering wheel. Why couldn't she figure it out?

TWENTY

Dark, dismal and distraught—that described Gabby's heart. No lights blazed inside the Ellison home, and it wasn't all that late. Gabby parked the vehicle and stepped out onto the paved circular drive. She and the girls had come to see Amber, while Clark vowed to track down the sheriff and try to get an update on the investigation.

"I don't think she's home," Rayne said.

Sheldon, with her taller stature, peered across the yard. "I don't see sign of anybody."

Gabby made her way up the large set of stairs to the veranda. After taking a deep breath, she pressed the doorbell.

Rhythmic chimes sounded, seeming to echo off empty walls.

Glancing around, Gabby took note of Robert's car parked just outside the closed garage. She pressed the button again.

"Come on, Gab. No one's here." Rayne nudged her.

"No. She's here."

Immy pressed closer to the door. "Do you hear anything?"

"No, but her only means of transportation is sitting outside the garage. That means she's home." Gabby pushed the doorbell a third time.

"Maybe she doesn't want company," Sheldon suggested.

"Then let her tell me." Gabby jabbed the button once more.

"That's out-and-out rude, Gabby Rogillio." Immy grabbed her arm and tugged. "Let's just leave the woman be."

Gabby sensed that Amber was just on the other side of the massive oak door.

Tonna and Sheldon started down the stairs. "Come on, Gabby. You can talk to her tomorrow."

Dragging her feet, Gabby turned to follow the girls down the steps.

Smash!

At the sound of glass breaking against tile flooring, Gabby spun around and crossed the veranda. She beat on the door with the side of her closed fist. The other girls hit it, as well.

"Amber, are you okay?"

"Let us in, Amber."

The dead bolt clicked, and Amber pulled the door open. She swayed as she moved out of its way. "Hey there, girls." Her words came out slurred.

Gabby pushed inside the house. The strong smell of liquor accosted her senses, making her take a step back. She fanned under her nose. "Amber, are you—" she leaned over to scrutinize the woman's face "—drunk?"

"Yep, I think I am." Amber nodded with slow exaggeration, then slumped against the door. As if in slow motion, she began to slide to the floor.

Sheldon whipped an arm around her waist, catching her. "Whoa, there."

"Let's get her to the couch," Immy said, her gaze glancing around the neighborhood outside.

They maneuvered Amber into the living room and Sheldon lowered her to the couch.

"What's wrong?" Immy sat beside the drunken woman.

"Well, let's see, Imogene. My husband's in jail for a crime he didn't commit, and my marriage is over anyway." She belched and giggled. "That's about it."

"I've never seen you drink before," Tonna said.

"That's because I never have. Not since high school, anyway." She bent her head and sobbed. "My whole life is one big mistake after another. No wonder everyone hates me. I should've just been shot a long time ago."

"That's not true." Immy patted Amber's knee. "God loves you and forgives you for every mistake you make. Forgiveness is His free gift. You only have to accept it."

Amber snorted. "You just don't know some of the things I've done. He, nor anyone else, could ever forgive me." Her sarcasm gave way to tears.

"Oh, He can always forgive. He knows we're sinners, one and all. The gift of salvation, of the promised eternal life, is yours for the taking. You simply have to admit you are a sinner and accept Jesus as your savior. He died on the cross for you." Immy's words were filled with such passion, tears welled in Gabby's own eyes.

"I don't think so. No one can forgive me for what I've done. Robert couldn't." She lifted her tear-stained face. "He really was planning on filing for divorce. He can't forgive what I've done." Her body shook as wave after wave of sobs tore from her. "And I love him so much."

Gabby knelt in front of her. "Is this about the baby you had with Sam and gave up for adoption?"

Amber's eyes went wide. "You know?"

"We found out today. Is that why Robert wants to divorce you? Because he found out you had a baby?"

"Not only that I had one and never told him, but because I gave it up for adoption." Fresh tears spilled from her eyes. "We tried to have children, but couldn't. For him to find out I gave one away…it was even worse." She sniffed. "After I had to tell him everything, he accused me and Sam of carrying on after we married. Said if I'd hide the fact that I'd had a child, I'd lie about an affair."

Gabby's heart twisted.

"I promise y'all, I never cheated on Robert. Not a single time. Never."

"We know you didn't, honey." Immy kept smoothing and patting, her words oozing like a soft balm.

"But he was even angrier about the money," Amber sobbed.

"Money?" Gabby's ears perked up and she rocked back on her feet. "What money?"

"The money I'd taken out of our accounts. Mine. Ours. The station's." She wiped her nose with the back of her hand. "Don't you see? I took out money from every account I could, and Robert found out. I don't know how I expected to hide it from him, but I just wasn't thinking. I was desperate."

Gabby jerked a tissue from the box on the end table and passed it to Amber. "Why would you do that? Why would you steal money from the station?"

"It all goes back to that horrible mistake. That child I gave up for adoption."

"I don't understand." Rayne moved to sit on her other side. "What does the baby you gave up have to do with you taking out money from the station's account?"

"The baby I gave up," Amber hiccupped, "is in town. He's been blackmailing me for the past six months. Threatening to expose me and my past. Threatening to tell everyone how horrible I am." She doubled over, sobs tearing from deep within her chest.

Gabby's emotions went off the radar. "Eric's been blackmailing you?"

Amber stopped crying and glanced up at her. "You know he's the baby I gave up?"

"We found that out today, too." Rayne shifted to face her. "He's been blackmailing you for money?"

"At first, I thought he just needed to know. He'd tracked me down, found his original birth certificate, made the connection between me and Jane." She swiped the tissue across her face. "I was happy to meet him, see that he'd been taken care of, but scared, too. Scared that Robert would see me with him and ask questions that would bring out the whole sordid story. My next mistake was telling Eric my fears."

Gabby squeezed her hands into balls until the nails digging into her palms hurt too much. "He started blackmailing you then? When he found out Robert didn't know you'd had a baby?"

"Yeah. He said he wanted to get Martin Tankersly back for all the abuse he'd endured, and he needed money to do it." New tears shimmered in her eyes. "I was heartbroken to hear of the abuse. If I'd known, I'd have never let Martin keep him after Jane died. Never."

"So you knew Eric was your son before he confronted you?" Gabby couldn't believe a woman would live in the same town with her own biological child and not try to cultivate a relationship.

"Of course. Jane was my cousin. Up until she died, she'd send me pictures and cards and such about him."

"But it was a closed adoption," Gabby argued.

Amber smiled. "We only did that to protect me. If someone had stumbled upon that information, it could have ruined me." Her smile turned sad. "Now it almost has. Can you imagine what the good folk of Mystique would have said? I'm sure they'll start up soon enough now."

"What about Robert? Didn't he have to know you'd just had a baby? I mean, you came back married pretty quickly," Sheldon stated.

The smile on Amber's face now reached her eyes. "I met

Robert two weeks after I'd had the baby and given it up. It was literally a fairy-tale romance. He swept me off my feet." Her eyes misted over again. "We spent every day together for a month, learning about each other and falling in love. I didn't tell him about the baby—after all, I didn't want to scare him off. I loved him more in that first month than the three years I'd spent with Sam." Her words trailed off, and she stared into blank space.

"But why didn't you tell him later?" Tonna asked.

"Because he proposed. I jumped at the chance." Amber shrugged. "I figured I would just let the past stay in the past and move forward with my life." She glanced around at each of the girls. "Don't you see? Robert made me special. He loved me for me, not because we'd become comfortable with each other. He wanted to marry me, to wake up next to me every morning for the rest of his life. That's intoxicating."

Gabby swallowed. How would it feel to wake up next to Clark for the rest of her life? The thought sent warm tingles through her body. It wasn't such a bad idea, maybe.

"We got married and he was looking to leave Louisiana, get out from under his parents' thumbs, so to speak."

"I can understand that," Rayne mumbled. Gabby's heart went out to her friend. Rayne had been living under the VanDoren shadow all her life.

"Naturally, I wanted to come home. Robert wanted to make me happy," Amber said, smiling wistfully. "So we moved to Mystique." She shook her head. "I didn't even think about how Sam would feel. I'm afraid he's always assumed Robert took advantage of me or something. He didn't. Truth be told, I took advantage of Robert's trusting nature."

Gabby shoved to her feet and paced, her steps moving as fast as her mind. "But you never told Robert about the baby? Even after you settled into marriage?"

"By then, it was too late. I mean, I hadn't realized how into the church he was. Oh, I knew he was a religious person when we dated, and he attended church all the time. I guess I just didn't realize how important it all was to him." She shook her head. "When we were dating in Louisiana, I pretended to be a Christian. But it was a lie. I couldn't look the preacher in the eye for fear God would reveal what I'd done." Amber lowered her voice another notch. "I still can't."

"But Robert's a deacon in our church. Of course, it's very important to him." Tonna shook her head. "And I just can't believe Eric would blackmail you."

"That's why I couldn't come clean later. Can you imagine how he'd have reacted if I'd told him sooner?" Amber's tears splattered from her eyes. "But I ended up having to tell him anyway, and look where it's got us."

"Why did you tell him?" Gabby turned to face Amber. "Why now?"

"I'd cleaned out all our personal accounts to pay Eric his blackmail money. I'm just lucky Robert bought out Howard before I emptied our accounts, or he'd have realized it sooner. But once all the money was gone, I had to come clean. I thought he'd forgive me."

"Why would you pay a blackmailer? Don't you know they just keep coming back again and again for more?" Sheldon asked.

"I was scared. Eric said he just needed some funds to try and get himself established. He needed to get away from his abusive stepfather. I had to help him, don't you understand? Not only to keep the secret from Robert, but also because I'd put my own son into such a horrible situation." She patted her eyes with the tissue. "I'm such a horrible person. A failure as a mother and a wife."

"So, you cleaned out your personal accounts. Then what?" Gabby probed.

"Eric said he had a plan. A way for Robert to never know the truth."

Gabby's compassion seeped away. Secrets and lies…murder.

"What happened then?" Tonna asked.

"I did tell Robert the truth. He blew up. Yelled and screamed. Accused me and Sam of carrying on all these years." Amber sniffed and blinked back the tears swimming in her eyes. "Told me he was going to divorce me and fire Eric. He wanted no part of the whole mess." The tears broke free and poured down her face.

"Great day in the morning."

"He wouldn't even look in my direction, much less talk to me. He'd sleep in the bedroom upstairs. Said he had an appointment with his lawyer." She wiped her nose on her sleeve, the tissue lying matted in her lap.

Frustration tightened on Gabby's stomach.

"But Eric told me he had a plan to protect me."

"What was that?"

"I went to him after Robert blew up. Eric said he could stop Robert from divorcing me. He said I would have total control of the station, and when that happened, I was to put him in charge."

Gabby couldn't wrap her mind around it. Why would Amber have trusted Eric at all? "And you went along with it? After he'd been blackmailing you?"

"He's my son. I don't expect any of you to understand. I was responsible for the abuse he'd endured from Martin Tankersly. I needed to help him. And I didn't want Robert to divorce me. Given time, we might've had a chance to work through it."

"What did Eric tell you?" Gabby held her breath.

"He didn't really tell me. After Howard was murdered, Eric called and told me to keep quiet. Said soon the station would be in my control. I'd save face in the community, and Robert wouldn't divorce me. I had no choice."

"We always have a choice," Sheldon snapped.

It all made sense now…the way Eric and Amber would never make eye contact…the way he tried to keep pointing the blame on Tankersly once he realized Gabby wouldn't stop searching until she found a way to clear Robert. He probably *did* call and ask his stepfather to come to the station to cast suspicion on him.

Gabby turned to Amber. "How does Howard fit into it?"

"Howard was suspicious of Eric…told Robert he should fire him. That's one of the reasons Robert and Howard argued, and why Robert bought out Howard. Over Eric, who wanted to put Martin to shame. Wanted him to live with knowing the stepson he'd always treated like a second-class citizen had bested him. Eric wouldn't be satisfied until he caused Martin's station to either close or have to sell to Eric."

Gabby held her breath, not believing what she was hearing.

Amber continued, her face contorted with pain.

"Eric planned to kill both Howard and Robert, thought he had. He shoved Robert and heard his head hit the stairs. Robert wasn't moving. He thought Robert was dead, so decided to frame him. He put the gun in Robert's hand and wrapped his finger through the trigger to get his fingerprints on the murder weapon." She lifted her face to the girls. "He's not really good at remaining calm."

Something was still off.

Amber sobbed softly. "All I know is that Eric told me if I opened my mouth about anything that would link him to the murder, I'd pay the ultimate price."

Gabby gasped. "Did you tell Sheriff McGruder all this?"

"I couldn't. I must keep quiet."

"Even though Robert could be charged for something Eric did?" Gabby couldn't keep the sharp tone from her words.

"I have to."

"No, you don't. You have to tell Sheriff McGruder this. Now." Gabby grabbed Amber's forearm and tugged her to her feet.

"You don't understand. I can't. I'll be divorced and an outcast. I'd be forced to move. There's nowhere for me to go anymore. I can't go back to my parents. They've never forgiven me for getting pregnant. And now that Mr. McKay has bought the station…well, Eric is desperate and there's no telling what he'll do. He's tried to scare off Mr. McKay already."

The vandalism. The trashing of his house. And once Gabby wouldn't give up digging, he'd slit her tires, called and threatened her. "You've got to stop thinking about yourself." Gabby moved her toward the front door. "You have to tell the truth and let the chips fall where they will."

Amber screamed. "I can't. I won't."

Then she collapsed into a crumpled heap on the tiled foyer.

TWENTY-ONE

Clark gripped the arms of the chair tighter. Fighting with Sheriff McGruder for the past hour and a half had worn him down. To top off his bad mood, the office reeked of burned coffee and stale air.

"I see where you're coming from, Mr. McKay, but I can't just bring Eric in for questioning. Being adopted isn't a crime." The small-town sheriff had long ago moved past Southern hospitality to just wanting Clark to leave. He'd asked flat out twice.

Too bad. Clark wasn't leaving until he got the man to agree to at least look into the evidence. "But Sheriff, just look at how it all links together. There has to be something missing, and isn't it your job to figure it out?"

"Look, I don't know how they did things from where you're from, Mr. McKay, but down here in Mississippi, we don't run around questioning innocent people." He leaned forward and rested his palms on his desk.

"But you'll lie in wait to lock up an innocent man, right, Sheriff McGruder?" a familiar throaty voice interjected.

Clark's heart rate increased as he jumped to his feet and turned. There she was—his vision of loveliness.

"Gabby, we've been through this all before." Sheriff McGruder rose to his feet, too much of a Southern gentleman to not stand when a lady entered the room.

But it wasn't just one lady who rounded the corner and filed into the sheriff's office. All of Gabby's friends marched in right behind her.

"Not this, we haven't." Gabby moved to stand beside Clark, and she took a second to give him a slow wink.

His heart quivered.

"What is it now?" The little lines around Sheriff McGruder's eyes etched deeper into his tanned face.

"We know who the real murderer is, as well as a blackmailer." Gabby threw a triumphant glare at the young lawman.

"Who would that be?"

"Eric Masters."

Clark didn't try to stop the smile from sliding across his face. They'd been right.

"All y'all got it in for Eric, huh?" The sheriff scratched the stubble on his chin. "I'm sure you're here to give me the same song and dance as Mr. McKay. But I'll tell you the same thing I keep telling him, it's not against the law to be adopted or work for your stepdaddy's rival business."

"How about blackmail and murder so you can get control of a radio station? Do those constitute crimes?" Sheldon moved from the back.

The sheriff rested his hands on his work belt. "What're you talking about, Sheldon?" His voice, unlike his earlier words, was softer, gentler.

Sheldon laid out facts like the librarian she was.

"Sheldon, you really do read too many of them mystery novels." But the sheriff wasn't laughing.

Neither were Gabby and her friends.

Sheriff McGruder scratched his chin. "How would Eric blackmail Amber Ellison? They hardly know each other."

"Maybe because he's the son she had right after graduation and gave up for adoption." Gabby smiled.

Sheriff McGruder fell back into his chair. "So Mr. McKay keeps claiming, but I just can't believe it."

Sheldon glared across the desk and wagged her finger at the sheriff. "It's true. We just got the whole truth from Amber Ellison. She's at home right now, worried about having to tell you all her painful secrets."

The heavy frown of the sheriff's face said it all. "I don't understand."

"I'm sure Amber will explain it all to you." Gabby crossed her arms over her chest.

She was really a little fireball when excited. Clark eased his hand around hers. She glanced down at him and squeezed. He couldn't wait to put this mess behind them and move into the future with Gabby at his side.

Thank You, Lord.

What would happen now that the sheriff knew the truth?

Gabby turned onto Sea Swept, her mind racing. McGruder had left the station in a hurry—to talk to Amber and then, if he felt it warranted it, to pay a visit to Eric. It would be. Finally, all the pieces fit together and soon Mystique could move beyond the secrets and tragedies.

After parking, Gabby headed toward the stairs of her apartment building. A silhouette stepped from the shadows, blocking her path. In the reflecting light from the parking lot, Eric stood before her, his face twisted into a menacing scowl.

Her heartbeat raced. Amber's evaluation that he was desperate echoed in Gabby's mind. She licked her lips with a dry tongue. "Eric, you startled me. What are you doing here?" She fought to keep her voice normal.

"You ruined my plans."

Play dumb. "What plans? What are you talking about?" She gripped her keys harder and made a move.

He stepped in her path. "Don't act stupid, Gabby. I know you know. I saw the sheriff going to visit my *mother*."

Every instinct told her to run…shout…anything, but she couldn't move. She had to think. Fast. "Eric, your mother's dead, remember?" Maybe she could confuse him.

He withdrew a gun from his jacket pocket and aimed it at her. "I had everything plotted out. Planned down to the T. McGruder bought it all. Everybody would've believed what I wanted them, had you just cooperated. But you couldn't do that. You had to keep digging, keep asking questions. Even the calls I made and slashing your tires wouldn't stop you." He took a step toward her. "You should've stopped."

She stumbled backward. "Eric, stop this. Let's talk about it."

"You and that uppity Mr. McKay. Y'all ruined everything. He'll get what's coming to him. As soon as I'm done with you."

Gabby's heart froze at the threat to Clark. In that moment, she knew two things for certain. One, she was well on her way to falling in love with Clark McKay. And two, she'd never get the chance to tell him.

God, please help me.

"Now I've got to leave town. Drop everything I've worked so hard to achieve." He moved closer. "All because of you."

Words failed her. It didn't matter—they wouldn't have been able to squeeze past the lump in her throat even if they'd formed.

No way could she make it up the stairs and into her apartment. He'd either tackle her or shoot her. Same scenario if she tried to run to her vehicle.

God, I need a miracle. Please, send me help.

Maybe the best defense was a strong offense. "Look, you could've told me what was going on. I could've helped you."

That stopped him. The gun wavered in his grip. "What? You? Miss Goody Two-shoes?" He made a sound that was half snort and half laugh. "Not hardly."

He'd called her bluff. Now, panic threatened to send her bolting, even though it'd surely bring a bullet to the back of her head.

Eric raised the gun again. "Where's your hospitality, Gabby? Aren't you going to ask me in?"

Bile seared the back of her throat. What would he do to her once he got her isolated in her apartment? The keys felt like cold steel against her palm.

She caught a flicker of movement on the steps behind him.

Clark eased his weight down to the last stair. His descent had been painstakingly slow, but he'd had to be silent. Seeing the fear on Gabby's face and hearing the desperation in her voice had nearly made him act too soon.

As soon as he'd seen Eric train the gun on her, he'd realized he loved her. With all his heart.

One more inch. Two. Silent. Careful.

From a crouching position, Clark rose in a flash, then pounced. His shoulder made contact with Eric's back as he lifted his arms under Eric's and slapped the gun out of the man's hands.

Eric turned on Clark. His eyes widened only a millimeter before he swung.

Clark dodged the blow, sidestepping. He countered with a left-right, making contact with Eric's chin and temple, then added a stiff kick to Eric's inner thigh.

Eric dropped to the ground.

Without hesitation, Clark jumped on top of him, using fists

to bring Eric under control. Every punch he delivered resonated inside him. This man could've taken Gabby from him forever.

Clark wouldn't have survived.

A siren wailed.

"I called the police while y'all were fighting." Gabby's voice crept through his fit of anger.

He pinned Eric's hands to the ground, straddling him. He fixed his gaze on Gabby.

She stared at him, trembling, but smiled. "The sheriff will be here any second."

He never wanted to hold anyone more.

The flashing lights atop the cruiser blinded him as it skidded to a stop. All he wanted to do was get to Gabby, hold her and tell her how much she meant to him.

Forever.

TWENTY-TWO

Morning in Mystique, with a murder solved and a man in her life, couldn't get any better.

Gabby smiled as she poured herself another cup of coffee and turned on the television set.

The camera zoomed in on Robert Ellison waving from the hospital door. A big smile split his face.

Robert Ellison awoke this morning to find his name cleared. Sheriff McGruder announced he and his staff uncovered new evidence, so the District Attorney's office has filed charges against a new suspect.

Gabby snorted. Puh-leeze. McGruder wouldn't have figured it out himself if a detailed novel had been left on his desk.

Sheriff McGruder, the man of the hour, was shown at the courthouse. Reporters flocked with microphones. "We have arrested Eric Masters in conjunction with the murder. No further information is available at this time."

Gabby punched off the television. At least Robert was cleared. That was good news, but having Eric attack her…well, it brought back all the memories from when she was attacked before. The difference now was that a man had risked his life to save her, not risked her life to save himself. She just had to keep reminding herself of that fact.

Her phone rang. She reached across the counter and grabbed the receiver. "Hello."

"Gabby, this is Amber Ellison. Did I wake you?"

"No, I was having coffee." Why would Amber call her?

"I guess you heard, huh?"

"I just saw the news. You must be excited."

"I'm scared. Did you talk to Imogene last night?"

"Not after we left the sheriff's office." Gabby had spent the better part of the night surrounded by her friends, sans Immy. The girls said Immy had been with Amber and Pastor Lum. "Why?"

"I gave my life to Christ last night."

"Oh, Amber. That's wonderful. I'm so happy for you." This was marvelous news indeed. Yes! Score another soul for God. Gabby suddenly had the desire to dance a jig in her pajamas in the middle of her kitchen. Go, God!

"I'm so peaceful." There was a long pause over the line. "But I'm scared Robert won't forgive me. Especially since I didn't come forward as soon as he was accused."

She had a point. Robert's name had been dragged through the mud because she hadn't spoken up.

"You know, Amber, you just have to put your faith in God. He's already got it all worked out according to His will."

"I know, but I'm still new at this trusting faith thing."

Gabby smiled. How well she remembered being a new Christian with so much to absorb. "I'll pray for you."

"I appreciate that, I really do, but…"

"But what?"

"I was just wondering if you could come over. Be here when Robert gets home. Let him know my accepting Jesus isn't just an act to get him to stay with me."

Great. She didn't want to be in the middle of their marital problems. However, by going to Amber with her questions the previous night, she'd pretty much plopped herself smack-dab in the center of their issues. Gabby switched off the coffeepot. "I'll get dressed and be right over."

Rushing to tug on a pair of jeans and T-shirt, Gabby reconsidered. Amber just needed moral support. Wasn't this what being a sister in Christ was all about—being there to support one another?

The drive across town and into the residential area of Mystique took Gabby a mere twenty minutes. She pulled her SUV into the circular driveway, past the magnolia trees in full bloom. Gabby slipped out of her vehicle and ambled to the stairs. Only Robert's car sat beside the garage. How was he going to get home from the hospital? Or worse, the courthouse? Sheriff McGruder was definitely the type to drag a man just awakened from a coma into police headquarters and make him give his statement.

Amber answered before the bell even finished its chime. "Thank you for coming." She motioned Gabby inside. She'd put on makeup, put a curl in her hair and wore a crisp pair of linen slacks with a silk tank top.

"You look nice." Gabby moved inside after giving her hostess a sideways hug.

"Thank you. I wanted to look nice for Robert." Amber played with the strand of pearls around her neck. "Would you like some coffee?"

"Please." Gabby followed her hostess into the kitchen. "Speaking of Robert, how's he going to get home?"

Amber's hands stilled over the cup she reached for. "I'm not sure. He didn't call." Her eyes widened and filled with tears. "You don't think he's not planning on coming home, do you?"

How was she supposed to answer that? "I don't know. Maybe the sheriff plans to bring him home." Discomfort wove around her spine, making her leg muscles burn to hightail it outta there.

"Oh. Right." Amber poured the coffee and pushed the cup toward Gabby.

Doctoring the java with about a thousand calories' worth of sugar and a heavy dose of real cream, Gabby smiled. What could she say?

God, please let him be planning to come home.

"Shall we wait in the living room?"

Gabby took a sip of the coffee before joining Amber. Rubbing a single pearl until Gabby thought it'd break loose of the choker, Amber then moved to the next one. Her movements were slowly grating on Gabby's nerves. "Tell me about your visit with Pastor Lum."

Clark finished finalizing his property deed in the Clerk of Court's office and headed for the front door.

"Mr. McKay!"

Clark turned. Robert Ellison rushed toward him. "Mr. McKay, I wonder if I might bother you for a ride home."

Why would the man ask him, of all people?

As if he could read Clark's mind, Robert flashed a smile. "Sheriff offered me a ride, but I had to decline. I just don't feel up to sitting in a police car for some strange reason."

"I can understand that. Sure, hop in."

"Thanks," Robert said as he opened the passenger door and pulled himself inside.

Clark slid behind the steering wheel and turned the engine over. He glanced at Robert, whose face carried a heavier weight than a man who had just had all accusations against him dropped should have.

"Is everything okay, Robert?"

"I hate that Howard was murdered." He shook his head. "It's

a waste. I still can't believe Eric killed him." Robert hesitated a long moment. "And I just don't know what to say to my wife."

"Look, it's none of my business, but I have to tell you, I think she was brave to come forward and tell the truth."

"Took her long enough."

"But she did."

"I suppose." Robert stared out the window. "I'm still angry for the deceptions, lies and stealing. Had I known from the beginning, maybe Howard would still be alive."

"You have every right to be angry. That's human nature." Why did the man pick him to talk to?

Robert stared at Clark. "It's human nature, but it's not spiritually correct. Is that what you're trying to say?"

The lump of discomfort doubled in Clark's throat. "Well, I know it's hard because we let emotions get all tangled up inside us." He shot a glance at Robert before directing his attention back to the road. The man didn't look mad. "I just try to remember that I make more mistakes than most, and I'm sure glad our Heavenly Father can forgive me so easily."

"I know." Robert leaned his head against the seat. "I know I should forgive Amber and move on. My heart, that's a totally different story."

"I can understand. It's a hard job."

The heat in the breeze was almost electrically charged. Something breathed over Mystique, something big.

Clark glanced over at the passenger's seat. Robert had his eyes clamped shut, but his lips moved. Praying. That was just what the man needed most, to go before the Lord and seek guidance.

Steering the car down Shannon Street, Clark looked again at Robert. His eyes were open and shimmering. "Thanks. I needed to be reminded of what I knew to be the right thing."

"God does like to use unlikely folks to give out His reminders sometimes."

"You know," Robert's smile widened, "you aren't so bad. For a Yankee and all."

Clark laughed as he turned in the driveway. Yep, Mystique had been the right choice for him. He slowed the car into the circular driveway as he rolled to a stop behind Gabby's SUV. What was she doing here?

"Looks like I have company." Robert stepped from the car.

"A welcome-home visit."

They reached the stairs, and Robert paused.

"Are you okay?"

"Yeah." Robert smiled. "It's just good to be home."

The front door swung open, and Amber Ellison stepped onto the porch. Her eyes were filled with tears and locked on Robert's face. She pressed fingers against her mouth.

Robert took the steps two at a time, holding out his arms. Amber rushed into his embrace. Their soft words tripped over each other—

"I'm so sorry."

"I understand."

"I love you."

"I love you."

Clark shifted his gaze to the flower bed, pleased the two would be okay, but very uncomfortable to witness their display.

"They'll work it out now," Gabby said.

He jerked his head. Clark glanced at the Ellisons. They were in a marital embrace. He smiled. "Yeah, I think they will."

"How'd you get the job of driving him home?"

Her spicy perfume vanquished the magnolia fragrance and did strange things to his pulse rate. He planted a soft kiss on her temple. "He didn't want to take the sheriff up on his offer of a ride."

"Can't say I blame him." She rested a hand against his check. "The bruise is gone now."

Heat that had nothing to do with the weather rattled him. He ran a hand through her hair, just gazing into her eyes.

"Why don't we get out of here and give them some privacy?" She held her hand out to him.

He wrapped his hand around hers, loving the softness of her skin against his. As if of one mind, Clark and Gabby stole silently to their vehicles.

TWENTY-THREE

Wʜat a blessed day!

Gabby squeezed Clark's hand under the crisp linen tablecloth at Ms. Minnie's. Their table felt cramped, but she was pleased to note that the girls had made room for Clark beside her.

The party to celebrate Robert Ellison's release—from the coma and from suspicion—was in full swing, just awaiting the arrival of the guest of honor. Ms. Minnie had done a beautiful job of decorating—balloons and streamers floated across the diner, and a big banner over the island bar read Welcome Back, Robert!

Gabby still had another hour before she had to go to work. David Gray had volunteered to work late so she could attend the first half of the party. Sitting beside Clark, surrounded by her best friends, Gabby couldn't imagine how she could possibly be any more content than she was at this moment.

The door swung open, and the Ellisons walked into the diner, arms linked. Applause erupted as townsfolk pushed to their feet. Amber's face flushed and her eyes teared up. Robert's mouth dropped open for a fraction of a second before a wide smile dug into his face.

Gabby jumped to hug them. "I'm so glad all this worked out. I'm happy for you."

"Thank you again for all you did." Robert patted her shoulder.

"I'd most likely be in jail if it weren't for you and your friends." He nodded toward Clark, hovering at Gabby's elbow. "And Mr. McKay here."

Robert and Amber finally made it to their table. Gabby's heart took a higher flight. This was what she loved about living in a small town—the sense of community, of belonging, of family.

The diner door flew open again, and Gabby darted her attention. She let out a little gasp as Sam Wood entered and trekked to Robert and Amber's table. Gabby jutted her chin in that direction. "Check that out."

Sam hovered over the table, his lips moving, but the noise was too intense in the diner for them to hear the conversation.

"Wish I was a fly on that table," Sheldon said.

Robert pushed back his chair and extended his hand to Sam. The men shook hands while Amber looked on.

"Guess all's well that ends well," Immy sighed as she straightened the silverware atop her napkin.

Robert dropped back into his chair, and Sam turned toward the girls' table. His steps were slow and slogging.

"He's coming this way. Wonder what he wants," Rayne whispered.

"Mr. McKay, ladies." Sam nodded as he stopped.

"Mr. Sam," a chorus answered.

"I just wanted to thank y'all for all you did. Getting everything out in the open was my wake-up call. Made me realize I needed to let go of the past." He jerked his thumb over his shoulder. "Those two are a good couple—they belong to each other. I've finally accepted that, and y'all helped me see that."

"I'm glad we could help, Mr. Sam." Immy waved toward the spare area of the table. "Would you like to join us?"

"No, ma'am. I just stopped by to wish Robert and Amber all the best. I'm on my way to the courthouse to see Eric."

Gabby nearly choked on her coffee. "You're going to see Eric?"

"Yes, ma'am. He's my son. I want to get to know him." His eyes misted over. "I didn't get a chance to know him growing up. I aim to change that now."

"I think that's wonderful, Mr. Sam," Immy said.

He nodded. "And Pastor Lum has agreed to give us some Christian counseling. He'll go to whatever prison Eric gets assigned to, and I'll go for all visitations."

"Oh, Mr. Sam, that's a great idea," Gabby said.

"Well, I just wanted to thank y'all. I'm much obliged." He gave another nod, then ambled out of the diner.

"Great day in the morning, things are looking up around here." Immy lifted her cup.

Gabby squeezed Clark's hand again. "Yes, they surely are."

"Oh, that reminds me." Rayne's eyes sparkled with excitement.

"What?" the other girls all asked in unison.

"Guess who's coming to the B and B next month."

"Somebody famous?" Tonna asked.

Rayne nodded. "Beverly Bates."

"The actress?" Sheldon squawked.

"The one and only." Rayne rubbed her hands together. "I can't believe it. She's actually going to be here, in *my* B and B. I'm beyond excited."

"That's awesome." Gabby shook her head—it wasn't every day Mystique got big-screen actresses coming to town.

"Her agent called this morning."

"Great day in the morning, why is she coming to Mystique?"

Rayne grinned. "Her agent said Ms. Bates was about to start work on her tell-all memoirs, and she'd hired someone in Mystique to do the ghostwriting." She tapped her finger against her tooth. "But with her entire entourage coming with her, I'm booked solid for the next month. It's great for business."

"Bet your dad is flipping out. Is he going to come to personally greet her?" Tonna asked.

"I haven't told him, and I don't intend to." Rayne's perfectly arched brows knitted. "This is really my chance to prove I can handle the business without his interference."

Immy stood. "I need to be heading out soon."

"Why?" the other girls all asked.

"I need to check on Mr. Tobias. He isn't doing so well."

"His Alzheimer's?" Tonna asked.

"It's not looking good for him."

Gabby shook her head and glanced at Sheldon. "So, have you talked to McGruder?"

"I think not." Sheldon stood and straightened. "I hate to be a party pooper, y'all, but I need to get home. I'm beat. I'll see y'all at church in the morning." She winked at Gabby. "And of course, I'll be tuning in to your show tonight."

Gabby glanced at her watch. "Oh, man, I need to get outta here. David'll wonder what happened to me."

Clark planted a kiss on her temple. "I'll be tuning in to your show, too."

Her heart flipped, pushed over by the spike in her pulse.

The final notes of the love song faded as Gabby queued up her microphone. "That was for Amber from Robert. Love well, you two. I'll be right back after these messages from our sponsors." She punched the button and leaned back in the chair as she nudged the headset down around her neck.

She laid the groundwork to air live calls on the turntable for the next segment. This was her favorite part of the night, when people would call in and she'd air them live, letting them send out their love dedications in their own words and voices. Even more so tonight, when her heart brimmed with happiness. While a lot of that had to do with solving the murder, Robert and Amber's reconciliation and Amber's salvation, Gabby knew in the depths of her soul that the main reason was because she had let go of her past experiences with Blake and moved on to her future with Clark.

The phone blinked. She waited until the commercials ended, welcomed her listeners back to the broadcast, then pressed the button to air the call. "KLUV dedications, you're on the air."

"Um. Yeah. I'd like to dedicate a song to a special lady." The man's voice was ragged, but familiar.

"Then you've dialed the right number. What song can I play for you?" Gabby spun her chair around. She'd have to work fast to grab the particular song and get it queued up before the caller finished his dedication.

"It's an older Elton John song." Why did his words seem forced?

"Great. I'm a huge Elton fan. What song?"

"'Sorry Seems to Be the Hardest Word.'"

She'd already moved to the Elton John section of her songs. Gabby pulled the request quickly. "An oldie, but a goodie. I'm assuming there's an apology dedication coming?" She hurried to get the song ready.

"Uh. Yeah."

"Want to tell me about it?"

"I told a lovely lady that I'd call her after our date. I got busy with work and then I thought too many days had passed, so I was scared to call by then."

"I can understand that." She had the song queued. "Go ahead and make your dedication directly to this lady."

"Okay. Um, Sheldon, I'm really sorry I didn't call you. I had a great time on our dates, and I'd love to be able to call you again. Uh, that's it."

Gabby sat in stunned silence for a moment, then jerked to attention. "And this is from?" As if she didn't already know.

"Harrison."

"This is for you, Sheldon, from Harrison." Gabby flipped the song to play and disconnected the call. Gabby bit back a smile. The sheriff may be a little slow on the draw, but it was sweet he'd publicly apologized to Sheldon in such a way. She just couldn't be sure about Sheldon's reaction…the woman had a mind of her own.

Her phone blinked again, even though the song wasn't even halfway over. "KLUV dedications."

"Did you put him up to that?" Sheldon's voice held no hint of teasing.

"No, I promise. He called on his own. Until he mentioned your name, I didn't even know it was him."

"Well, one of you girls had to put him up to it. He wouldn't think to do it himself."

"Come on, Shel, the man's smitten. It was a nice gesture." The countdown clock clicked to sixty-two seconds.

"No, I can't accept that. It's so unlike him. I'm calling Immy. If I find out she put him up to this…"

Gabby's other line blinked. "Just calm down, Shel. He did it himself and that took a lot of guts to make such a public apology." Countdown marked twenty seconds flat. "I've got to go, Shel. We'll talk about this tomorrow."

"You bet we will."

She kept her eye on the countdown clock. When it reached eight seconds, Gabby reduced the volume on the last notes of the song and answered the new call. "KLUV dedications, you're on the air."

"I have a very special dedication request tonight." Clark's smooth voice sent her heart thumping.

"You do, sir?" Gabby couldn't stop the smile from creeping into her voice. The man just made her giddy, plain and simple.

"Oh, yes." His laughter seeped into his words.

"What song would you like to dedicate tonight?" She spun around and poised her hand to pull the song.

"Celine Dion's 'Because You Loved Me.'"

Her heart twisted as she automatically reached for the song. "And your dedication?" Her voice hitched while she moved to queue up the song.

"Oh, this goes out to you, Gabby Rogillio. Because the first time I laid eyes on you, the first time I knew for sure that beauty from the inside out existed, I knew I wanted to be a better man because of you. And I am. Because you love me."

She paused, no words slamming into her mind.

"And because I just received word that your show is being syndicated."

Oh, now she really *was* speechless.

"And then there's this whole house thing." His voice sounded huskier.

"House thing?"

"I have this beautiful house that's entirely too big for a bachelor. I'm looking for someone to spend the rest of my life with. Someone who'll be my special blessing from God."

Gabby couldn't think straight. She queued up the song and clicked his call off the air. "Clark?"

"Yes, darling?"

She chuckled. "Uh, Yankee, that's pronounced *darlin'*."

His laughter filled every available space in her heart. "Okay, yes, *darlin'*?"

"Why don't you come visit me? I have this overwhelming urge to give you a great big hug."

"Why don't you look out the studio door, *darlin'*?"

Gabby dropped the phone and rushed out of the studio. Clark held a bouquet of white Confederate roses in one hand, the other had a cell phone pressed to his ear.

As she moved into his arms, her heart began to sing the sweetest of love ballads ever written.

* * * * *

Dear Reader,

My mother was born in Mississippi, so I had no choice but to set a book in the state. What a journey my research took me on. I hope you enjoyed visiting my fictional coastal town of Mystique as much as I did creating it.

Gabby and Clark were such fun characters to write. The supporting cast of Gabby's friends filled me with laughter at times, and brought me near to tears, as well. Through it all, I pray that the storyline touched you in some way, and left you feeling the hope and promise of the future.

I love hearing from readers. Please visit me at: www.robincaroll.com and drop me a line, or write to me at: PO Box 242091, Little Rock, AR, 72223. Join my newsletter group…sign my guestbook. I look forward to hearing from you.

Blessings,

Robin Caroll

QUESTIONS FOR DISCUSSION

1. Gabby's past troubles with a relationship left her wary, which could have cost her Clark's love. Have you ever had something from your past interfere with your current relationships? How did you handle it?

2. Amber let a situation get out of hand because she was concerned, in part, about her reputation. Have you or someone you loved ever had to live down a reputation? How did you deal with the situation?

3. Clark felt like an outsider in Mystique at first. Have you ever felt that way? How did you work through your feelings?

4. Gabby jumped to conclusions a lot and was proved to be wrong. Have you ever done something similar? Explain.

5. Clark purchased the house Gabby had her heart set on, and it disappointed her greatly. Have you ever felt that way? How did you reconcile your emotions?

6. Martin Tankersly was a surly old man who made a lot of people's lives miserable. Have you ever had to deal with someone close to you with those character traits? How did you handle the relationship?

7. Clark felt that he was put into a no-win situation. Have you ever been in a similar situation? What did you do?

8. Law enforcement doesn't always get it right. Have you ever been convinced law enforcement was wrong in a particular situation? How did you handle that in a Christian manner?

9. Robert was accused of a crime he didn't commit. Have you ever been falsely accused of something? What did you do?

10. Gabby and Clark had to learn to trust each other in order to claim love. How important is trust to you in your personal relationships?

11. Gabby went back and forth about Robert's innocence. Have you ever argued with yourself about another person? What happened?

12. Gabby's friend, Tonna, is a gossip at heart. How have you dealt with gossips?

13. Gabby leaned on her friends throughout the book. Do you have friends you can count on through any trial? Are you a friend like that to someone else?

14. Eric acted out once he found out he was adopted. Do you know someone who's adopted? How does his or her experience differ from Eric's?

15. In the end, Sam was able to forgive Amber and accept Eric. How do you handle forgiveness?

When his niece unexpectedly arrives at his
Montana ranch, Jules Parrish has no idea what
to do with her—or with Olivia Rose,
the pretty teacher who brought her.
Will they be able to build a life—and family—together?

Here's a sneak peek of "Montana Rose"
by Cheryl St.John,
one of the touching stories in the new collection,
TO BE A MOTHER,
available April 2010
from Love Inspired Historical.

Jules Parrish squinted from beneath his hat brim, certain the waves of heat were playing with his eyes. Two females—one a woman, the other a child—stood as he approached.

The woman walked toward him. Jules dismounted and approached her. "What are you doing here?"

The woman stopped several feet away. "Mr. Parrish?"

"Yeah, who are you?"

"I'm Olivia Rose. I was an instructor at the Hedward Girls Academy." She glanced back over her shoulder at the girl who watched them. "My young charge is Emily Sadler, the daughter of Meriel Sadler."

She had his attention now. He hadn't heard his sister's name in years. *Meriel.*

"The academy was forced to close. I thought Emily should be with family. You're the only family she has, so I brought her to you."

He took off his hat and raked his fingers through dark, wavy hair. "Lady, I spend every waking hour working horses and cows. I sleep in a one-room cabin. I don't know anything about kids— and especially not girls."

"What do you suggest?"

"I don't know. All I know is, she can't stay here."

*Will Olivia be able to change Jules's mind
and find a home for Emily—and herself?*

*Find out in
TO BE A MOTHER,
the heartwarming anthology from
Cheryl St.John and Ruth Axtell Morren,
available April 2010
only from Love Inspired Historical.*

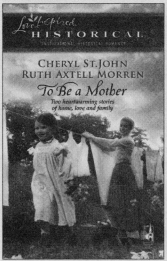

LARGER-PRINT BOOKS!

GET 2 FREE LARGER-PRINT NOVELS PLUS 2 FREE MYSTERY GIFTS

Love Inspired®

SUSPENSE
RIVETING INSPIRATIONAL ROMANCE

Larger-print novels are now available...

Love Inspired
SUSPENSE

TITLES AVAILABLE NEXT MONTH

Available April 13, 2010

ON THIN ICE
Whisper Lake
Linda Hall

DEADLY VOWS
Protecting the Witnesses
Shirlee McCoy

CALCULATED REVENGE
Jill Elizabeth Nelson

MOUNTAIN PERIL
Sandra Robbins

LISCNMBPA0310